The Mares of Lenin Park

The Mares of Lenin Park

a novel by

Agustin D. Martinez

Hollywood Books International
Hollywood, California

Published by
Hollywood Books International
the fiction imprint of Press Americana
the press of

Americana:
The Institute for the Study of
American Popular Culture
7095-1240 Hollywood Boulevard
Hollywood, CA 90028

http://www.americanpopularculture.com

Cover Art: Franz Marc, The Large Blue Horses, 1911

Library of Congress Cataloging-in-Publication Data

Martinez, Agustin D.
The mares of Lenin Park : a novel / by Agustin D. Martinez.
pages cm
ISBN 978-0-9829558-5-7
1. Teenage boys--Fiction. 2. Fathers and sons--Fiction. 3. Refugees--Cuba--Fiction. I. Title.
PS3613.A786385M37 2013
813'.6--dc23
2013003177

PROLOGUE

The following story is fact – for the most part. There's no need to get into which parts are fact and which are true; there is a difference you know! Besides, my story may be flushed with the hues of veracity that have colored my life ever since I arrived in Miami back in 1992. I've learned quite a bit living here in Miami – a refugee among exiles – and I've fallen victim to remembering my past through the eyes of those exiled here who tell our Cuban story much more resplendently than I could ever tell it or remember it.

Since arriving in America, I've learned a lot about whom I was and what I was lacking in Cuba, and this, no doubt, has been archived in my brain as true and correct. I've also learned that the "special era" I believed to live in was merely an illusion the bearded one conjured and summoned decades before I was born.

So you see, just like an artist's mound of clay, truth can be molded. It can be shaped with whatever dreams, wishes, or must've-beens swirl in one's head. So, again I ask that you won't judge me for any gaps I may have left out or for any details that may seem a bit stretched to you. It's human nature to stretch things a bit – especially if you're Cuban!

Even though I thought I had it all figured out, my first English teacher in the United States taught me a very important lesson regarding truth and fact. Soon after arriving on the shores of Miami, I was asked to describe my hometown of Havana in a well-structured, five-paragraph essay. If my English teacher, Mrs. Sánchez-Medina, and the principal, Dr. Méndez-Delgado, gave it a thumbs-up, I would have the privilege of reading it at *Noche de Orientación.*

It would be a good melodramatic opening for the meeting that would honor Dr. Vázquez-Díaz, Miami-Dade County Public Schools Superintendent, who was trying to clean up his image after the embezzlement charges that showed up in *El Nuevo Herald.* Like Mrs. Sánchez-Medina, Dr. Vázquez-Díaz believed that fact and truth were dissimilar.

1

"What would be better than having an immigrant, newly-arrived to the diaspora, saluting the American flag, perhaps shedding a tear of joy, and reading an essay in broken English?" they both explained in their best Spanish possible. My reading would be preceded by the modern dance class's "Dances of Cuba."

I was told that the Public Relations firm of Ferrer & Associates was aiding in promoting this event around the community for free, and they would need me to do a voiceover so they could provide the media with effective sound bites. I also heard that el maestro, Cachao – the real Mambo King – would stop by, if he had time, to surprise the modern dance class. What a night they had planned!

Then, parents would be asked to join the PTA and contribute as much as they could to help poor refugee balseros like me. Even though my accent has always been pretty good, better than many of my English teachers in Miami I might add, I would play it up for the crowd when necessary, leaving out a few articles, making H's guttural, or pronouncing I's like double E's. After all, everyone's heart was set on what I personified. I was the tired and the poor that the Statue of Liberty asked for.

Everyone looked forward to the catharsis that would tsunami over the Miami Springs Sr. High auditorium.

My part was easy, they assured me. Mrs. Sánchez-Medina and the rest of the audience members, those who remembered a bright and vibrant city, a city that had only become blinding in its splendor when filtered through their memories, wanted to hear that modern-day Havana had been plunged into dark and dust, smelling of dead carcasses and inequities. Perhaps some of them even pictured turkey vultures soaring ominously over the pestilence while the wind whistled with the moans of the dearly departed that would never set foot on the island again.

Everyone at Miami Springs Sr. High wanted me to tell them how lucky they were to have made the wise decision to leave decades earlier so their progeny wouldn't have to witness the blight and destruction Castro inflicted on our people. They wanted me, a fourteen-year old cubanito, to assure them that

2

there was no need to feel any guilt over having left their homeland decades ago.

Even though at this point in my life I couldn't imagine living in any other country besides the USA, *my* Havana was mesmerizing. Moreover, I didn't see a reason to choose between my two loves, my two countries that I straddled on a daily basis.

How could I express this without causing a cataclysmic effect on the young urban Cuban-Americans – or YUCAs as they were known in the city – who would be listening to my oral presentation on the edge of their seats, their starched handkerchiefs waiting to sop up any tears that overflowed?

I could just imagine the principal, counselors, and the rest of the YUCAs applauding with tears streaming down their faces as I told them what they wanted to hear, and this was quite motivating, just as motivating as the good grade I was sure to receive.

I wanted to tell them that the streets cried with their childhood memories while peanut vendors sang *¡Maní, maní caliente!* as they passed out warm peanuts in day-old *Granmá* newspaper cones to children who hadn't eaten a good meal in weeks.

They would surely want to hear that their homeland no longer looked like the pictures at Versailles restaurant in Little Havana on Miami's *Calle Ocho*, those pictures taken so many lifetimes ago. Actually, the streets *did* look like those pictures because nothing had changed. Buildings, signs, and even the occasional Fords and Chevys still lined the streets like on an abandoned set of an old 50's flick, paint flaked a bit on the walls, with a brick or two missing here and there.

I wanted to tell Mrs. Sánchez-Medina that modern-day Havana was the worst place on earth. I really, truly did since that would have made her day. But none of that was true. It wasn't the worst place on earth, even though it no longer felt like what a home should feel like. I was willing to perform to their expectations, even willing to act as melodramatically as I could – I'm pretty good at that – but I couldn't just lie for the sake of it.

During my teacher's mandatory brainstorming activity worth fifteen points, all I could think of were the stories my

3

grandmother told me as a kid, of the parties before the Revolution, with American movie stars and diplomats wearing their expensive furs – although it rarely dropped below 22°C.

Cuba reminded me not so much of those legendary parties as much as the morning after when everything's a mess. You know, furniture's chipped, perhaps a cigarette burn on the carpet. That wasn't destruction; it was merely a vivid memory that something fun, alive took place, no matter how indulgent. It was like Mardi Gras – one last hoopla before solemnity struck midnight.

Walls of buildings in Havana yellowed. The Fifth Avenue sidewalks acquired a look of melancholy with their cracked memories of foreigners who would never return to help clean up the mess. The royal palm trees withered a bit and went to sleep only to dream of the mythical Havana of the fifties. That's how my neighborhood in El Vedado looked when I left in '92. One giant hangover!

Neither politics nor economics popped into my head after completing my next ten-point prewriting activity for Mrs. Sánchez-Medina's essay. The image that continued possessing my hand as I wrote was that of a silent ballroom just after a celebration, the deep silence that follows a shattering wine glass, the kind of silence that makes you hold your breath while your heart beats out of your chest for what seems like an eternity. But I guess I didn't convey that too well. Apparently, although it was not on the rubric, politics and failed economics were the key points to be made in my assignment.

I got a "C" for writing only four paragraphs. You see, "a fifth concluding paragraph would brace my story," and, consequently, I was not invited to read my essay at the school's *Noche de Orientación*. Instead, Arturito read his poem, a poem that didn't even rhyme!

My teacher derided me. She said that I shouldn't be afraid of speaking the truth. That admitting how much I despised my communist country wouldn't ensue in *militantes* knocking down my door. I was in America now, and everyone knew how horrible it was back home, and how we were brainwashed into

4

turning in our relatives who spoke against the State just for a few erasure marks on our ration cards.

The principal called me into his office and told me I needn't write *Castrista* propaganda like that at his school, but his scolding was soon interrupted by his cell phone ringing, letting him know his reservations at The Strand were confirmed. He was quite relieved and forgot about me altogether. After all, Pilar was performing her one-woman keyboard act by the bar. Her version of "Yellow Mango" always put everyone in a jubilant mood.

It was amazing to me that my critics in Miami were judging my experience even though they themselves had never been on the island! Then it clicked. Genetic memory.

Back in Havana, I heard of this experiment with baby chicks. The chicks were allowed to roam, just pecking and shitting. Shadows were projected overhead – shadows of jays, airplanes, cardinals, you get the picture.

The chicks just went along with their lives like nothing. But when shadows of chicken hawks panned across the wall, the baby chicks reacted. Their little heads popped up and they ran in circles, completely panic-stricken; some even died of fright.

Yet, the chicks had never seen a chicken hawk before. There weren't even any adult chickens in their small scientific pens with them to teach them they should be scared to death of the predator scoping out a meal from far above. The chicks knew to be afraid because it was written in their DNA. Survival was part of their very makeup, their building blocks, passed from mother hen and father rooster to chick.

Perhaps Cubans in the diaspora had developed some sort of genetic memory that they passed down to their descendants in the same way. This adopted nostalgia must have been completely biological. It allowed third- and fourth-generation Cuban-Americans to remember passionately what Cuba was like – how velvety *mantecado* ice cream melted on their tongues, the rich pungent odor of pre-Castro coffee, how sweet the fried plantains were and how the caramelized, burnt edges stuck to their teeth – and yet their families had lived in other countries for generations

5

and the only Spanish they could muster was to ask *Abuelita* for more *café con leche* and toast.

Perhaps our people developed this genetic memory to allow us to know the moment we're born, before we even open our eyes, before our first feeding, where home truly was and how cruel life was for exiling us from paradise, a paradise once devoid of shadows, devoid of chicken hawks.

CHAPTER 1

It all started on my mother's wedding day. The doubts that is, the doubts that even though I couldn't imagine living anywhere else, being anything but Cuban, things no longer felt . . . right. In the midst of that humid and stormy day, Graciela looked like Our Lady herself. Her chestnut eyes gleamed like never before. Graciela looked like a porcelain doll dressed up as a bride for some little girl to play with as she imagined her own wedding day far off in the future. The humidity condensed on Graciela's glistening olive skin, giving her an incorporeal look, one that I couldn't help but worship.

I had to admit she chose a good time to get married. The city's morale was quite high that April being that the Eleventh Pan-American Games were going to be held in Havana. *El Comandante* was quite certain that these games were going to bring in the necessary currency and publicity needed to maintain the Revolution's goals. It seemed that everyone agreed, but in fact everyone was just anxiously awaiting the spectacle of the festivals, the waving flags, and the flashing bulbs of the cameras that would blind the island of the reality awaiting them back on their city block.

So there would be some more publicity. Was that really a good thing? More publicity to show the world how badly we lived. More publicity to show the world that Cubans weren't going to give up their homage to the bearded one, no matter what. More publicity to show the nations of the twentieth century how Cubans survived on dreams and principles of former generations while hunger secretly panged in our bellies.

I had never disagreed with the bearded one before; in fact, it had never occurred to me that I even *could*. It seemed only a handful of us were left in the city who actually wanted to continue striving for the challenges placed on us in this special time.

It was just that lately, with all the American dollars flowing in from Cubans in the outside world, the TV cameras, the foreign reporters – I don't know. It just seemed that *El Líder* was growing senile or greedy and forgot about the promises he made to himself, to us, and to the rest of the world who believed him and believed that his country was striving for something righteous.

I didn't share this with Nestor, my cousin and best friend in the whole wide world. It's not that he would have turned me in or anything. He would have probably just told me to wake up and accept the fact that we had to go along with whatever antics our President planned. After all, this was our fatherland. Nestor would have slapped me on the back of my head and told me to stop thinking so much. He was right. My mind often went on and on making me say things and do things I wouldn't have done if passion hadn't gotten the better of me.

Besides, I was simply a kid and didn't share the wisdom of *El Comandante* and our forefathers. Perhaps the Pan-American Games *would* dignify the island and help my comrades feel that patriotic fervor once more. Perhaps the foreign currency was somehow justified by some sub-clause in our constitution, which I never did have the opportunity to read, now that I think about it.

By now, nobody cared about the Revolution, its principles, or its demands. My comrades just coveted American dollars and foreigners and pretended never to have been part of Castro's ideals. Maybe *El Líder* was as wily as I always took him to be. He knew these games, the zeal of preparing our Cuban compatriots to outrun, outswim, and outride athletes from around the globe, would be just what we needed to boost our economy and our spirits. Perhaps these accomplishments would unite us once again. No more us and them on our own island, just *us*. I hoped he was right. I often felt alone and a fool. But I wouldn't give up. Better days were ahead; they had to be. Our forefathers promised.

I didn't mind the ration lines all that much; I had never known anything else. I didn't even mind having to gather wounded birds so that we could have something to put in the mock Galician stew. Even when it came to the *trabajo voluntario*, although there was nothing voluntary about it, I knew it was my duty to "voluntarily" attend summer camp.

What bothered me was that we hid these and so many things from the rest of the world, as if *El Comandante* was ashamed of the Revolution's demands on its people. Consequently, shame gushed down to us from above, and I supposed this is why so many of my comrades gave up our revolutionary plight.

If only we could have been open with the world from the beginning and showed everybody how Cubans sacrificed themselves by riding thirty-year-old *camellos* packed at three hundred percent capacity, or how we walked five kilometers for two plantains and a few grams of coffee, or how we panicked when we misplaced our *libreta*, the rations booklet that would take months to replace, I don't think people around the world would judge us the way they do.

Nevertheless, ploys like having the Pan-American Games here is what kept my comrades going. They fantasized meeting foreigners who would revitalize the Cuban economy. Foreigners to father and sustain our babies. Foreigners with the magic and wisdom to turn our home into the heavenly city of lights it once was.

Inasmuch as I wanted my mother to postpone the wedding, Cuba was on a lucky streak and that was that.

"Don't you have any face powder?" my mother, Graciela, asked my bucktoothed cousin Beatriz who was touching up the bride's makeup. Graciela's high cheekbones needed no makeup to highlight their contour, but that was my biased opinion. Her full Creole lips needed no ruby lipstick to enhance their plumpness either. But there would be pictures taken, and a Cuban bride couldn't be photographed without makeup, no matter how perfect her visage.

9

The rain's raucous seemed to make everyone more nervous. Beatriz dashed out of the room to find the bride some more face powder. She thought she had brought enough makeup from the mortuary where she worked, but she was clearly running out. Reminding my mother that rain was a good omen, Beatriz found some baby powder that she ended up mixing with the little translucent face powder that remained.

"Rain means prosperity, rebirth," she told my mother, nodding her head up and down while she mixed the powders on a piece of overused wax paper, her two front teeth pressing hard onto her crushed bottom lip.

Graciela didn't care for omens, and she continued dressing, pushing her arms through each faux-pearl-crocheted sleeve. The sleeves weren't the problem; it was her Cuban hips that made getting into the dress difficult.

The wedding was supposed to start half an hour ago, but everyone was running late due to the April torrents. It was bad enough that they were on Cuban time, too. You know, about half an hour late. So between the storm and the usual Cuban fear of being the first one to arrive at any party, I was surprised a wedding even took place that day.

The exposed sixty-watt bulb hanging from the ceiling flickered, and I prayed the lights would go out. They rarely stayed on even in good weather. And although the power went out at least twice a day, due to our aggressive energy conservation plan some said, it was just my luck we weren't conserving any electricity that day even with a squall beating down the power lines.

The bridesmaids, hovering around Graciela like hummingbirds, were agitated that I was in their way, moving me this way and that, asking me to stand over here and over there like some superfluous pigeon-shit-covered statue at Lenin Park. Perhaps there was still *something* I could have said that would have shined some light on the catastrophe about to take place, so I wasn't moving from my mother's side. I felt like I hadn't said enough, like she didn't understand what marrying the doctor was doing to me and to the memory of my dead father, Ulises Aguilera.

10

I was the only boy in the room, but I didn't mind. The bridesmaids signaled each other with their eyes every time they said something they didn't think appropriate for me to hear. I simply pretended to be a fourteen-year-old who didn't understand what they were saying. It made everyone feel more at ease since they thought I just didn't understand girl talk.

"Doesn't she look beautiful?" winked Aunt Cecilia. "She looks like an angel. Doesn't she, Uli?"

"She looks too good for that monster," I blurted without thinking. Too many instances occurred when I thought one thing and my mouth said another. My cousin Nestor used to remind me to "think twice before speaking – and then just don't speak." But there I went, "You shouldn't be sleeping with that monster!"

Some of the women chuckled out of nervousness. Graciela darted a glance at their direction.

"*¡Basta!*" Graciela shouted. "I can't believe...not today, Uli, *por favor*." Turning to Ana-Belkys, "The bouquet, where's the bouquet?" My mother nervously patted the vanity table.

"It's right here," Aunt Cecilia immediately responded in her calming voice, pointing to the bouquet made of butterfly jasmine, yellow bells, and a few blossoms from an octopus tree. "Just relax, my darling," her sister said, wiping the humidity off the bride's forehead. They gave each other a strong hug, and my uncle's waving hand from outside told everyone that it was time to proceed with the ceremony.

"I never thought the day would come," teary-eyed Cecilia whispered to my mother. They hugged once more and Cecilia left the room yelling to her husband, "Francisco, *¡Ya estamos listas!*"

"I'd like a moment alone with Uli," my mother advised her ladies-in-waiting. "It'll only be a second."

This was my chance. This was when I had to say everything just as I planned, everything I had forgotten to say before. *Think! Think!* The women said their farewells and patted me on the head or pinched my cheeks, conveying only with their eyes for me to watch what I say. Beatriz looked at me with the dumbest look, her painted eyebrows raised, her protruding buckteeth crushing her bottom lip in the usual way.

11

"Uli, I want you to know that I love you more than anything in this world," my mother began.

"I know," I answered in a defeated tone. Maybe she'd feel sorry for me and cancel the wedding. That was childish, stupid, and ineffective. Instead of causing her grief, I just eased her mind.

"Antonio is a good provider," she said. "He'll be a good father."

"I have a father! What about *Papi*?" I confronted her with the memory of my father, her dead husband. "What about him?"

"Oh, Uli, he's been gone an awful long time. You say you remember him, but you were too young. He went to fight a war…"

"…for his country, for us!" I interrupted, afraid of what she was going to say next. "That's all I need to know."

"You're old enough to understand that it's very hard for a woman to be without a husband in Havana. Things are really difficult for us," she tried to convince me.

"So *I'll* make sure that you have everything we need. Just you and me! I make the ration lines, ask around to see what trucks are coming in before the rest of the city finds out." The thunder cracked louder making the whole room shake and light up in a flash.

"There'll be a lot less lines to make now that Antonio is with us. He's got connections that will make life so much easier for us. I doubt you'll have to make *any* ration lines again."

"What's the point of not making lines?" I shrugged, not wanting to admit what a great relief this would be. "What will I do all day when all my friends are standing in lines? I got nothing better to do, anyway."

"The things you say," she smiled, trying to assuage the tension. "I don't think the ration lines are what you're worried about. Do you think your father…"

"He still visits me at night, you know," I reminded her in case she had forgotten the last time I woke up sweating and screaming.

12

I didn't tell her that last night I dreamed he was still alive and didn't know how to get home. He had lost his memory in Angola and forgot where he came from. I yelled and yelled, but he didn't hear me. I told him to continue walking towards me, but he just looked around while missiles flew overhead and corpses reached skyward, one even grabbing his pant leg to avoid being sucked into limbo.

It always took me a while when I woke up to acknowledge which parts were dreams and which parts were true; yesterday was mostly a dream, though. But sometimes, no kidding, he really did come to my room and speak to me. He was proud of the way I took care of my mother. He was proud of how well I read from the State school books. Sometimes I would even read him some Lefebvre or Engels. He loved philosophy, my uncle once told me.

"Uli, enough. We've talked about those dreams."

"They're not dreams, *Mami*. Fortuna said they're apparitions."

"They're all in your head, honey. Keep talking like that and you'll find yourself in a *manicomio* on the other side of the island."

"If they're in my head, why did you take me to Fortuna's? You asked her to cast a bunch of cowry shells on a mat and spit tobacco juice all over the statue of *San Lázaro*. If it's all in my head, why'd we bother? You know *Papi* has been visiting me because he wants to make sure we're all right."

"Ulises, we all believe things we need to believe in times of..." the bride stopped knowing the wheels in my head were turning with what I'd say next and wasn't listening to a word she was saying.

"He's gone, baby. He's gone. Forget what that superstitious Fortuna tells us. She doesn't know what she says sometimes. She's getting old, *Papito*. Look, you should be very proud of your father and let him rest," she said, ignoring Fortuna's prophecies of what would happen to us if I didn't bathe in *agua florida* to cleanse me spiritually and appease the *Orísha*.

13

I stood up behind my mother and looked at her through the oxidized mirror. I looked increasingly like my father's picture every year, broad shoulders and all. I knew my mother could see that through the smoky glass; it frightened her. My eyebrows had blackened and thickened much like his. The strong Aguilera chin had developed nicely, giving my face a square definition. Like two Greek olives, my eyes stood out, feathered by the long lashes my mother found so striking in my father.

We stood parallel to each other's image discussing the visions of my father through the piece of foggy mirror held up by two rusty and mangled clothes hangers. Clearly, the bride had given up waiting for her husband to return, but I wasn't ready to give up a father I hardly even knew. It simply wasn't fair. Maybe he was still lost at sea; maybe somebody bewitched him so he would lose his memory.

"You've done an excellent job, Ulises," my mother continued, trying to ease my giving her away. "And you'll continue giving me the kind of love only you can give me. But I need to think of me too, Uli," she said, wincing her eyes which created a concave pyramid on her forehead.

"Are you willing to give me that?" When I didn't respond and just stared back through the mirror, "Well, I'm willing to do this for *me*. I've been the brave widow, living up to everyone's expectations of what a hero's wife should be," she said dusting my hair back out of my face.

"I held my head up high at too many processions, accepting medals from generals who never even knew your father. No one asked if I could do it; no one asked if I needed any time by myself. Not once did I think of me! I don't want any more plaques; I don't want to hear another speech about a husband who is never coming back," she paused, looking at the ground for some other way to convey the threshold she had reached. "I just want to stop hurting. Antonio makes me forget the pain."

"Your father would've been very proud of the way I handled myself. Sitting at night alone. Wondering if he would miraculously just walk in through the front door to surprise us that he was back. It's time for me to have someone, don't you

14

think? Not someone to replace your father," she whispered grabbing my hand. "I don't think there's a man on the island who can do that. But it's time for me to walk out into the street and smile and say I'm in love. It's time for me to laugh like I used to laugh. I've been desperately lonely, Uli. You're grown up enough to understand that. And it's time I feel alive. It's time I walk into the light and bathe in its warmth without remorse."

"I was there," I quickly reminded. "I was there right beside you."

"I don't have the energy anymore, Uli. I've been an admirable mother, a loyal widow. I dealt with the accusations of your father being a spy and…"

"He wasn't a spy!" I shouted into the smoky glass. The wind and rain continued beating down the sidewalks of El Vedado.

"Of course he wasn't a spy," she laughed. "But remember how they accused him? Evil men who wanted to shame his grave. Evil men who wanted to shame his bed. Yet I stood there waiting to suffer whatever consequences…"

"What does that have to do with this wedding?" I asked, truly wanting to know how my father's memory was the impetus for her marrying the doctor.

"These are very hard times. *Ese mango verde* has been promising that things will get better since I was your age, and…" she cut herself off knowing it was anything but sagacious to discuss these antisocial feelings even with her own son or to call our President a "green mango" that would never fall off the proverbial tree of politics. "These are very hard times," she just repeated.

"This is a special time," I tried reminding her, but Graciela just wasn't listening. "Be brave," I told her. "Hang on to the Revolution's dreams! That's what *Papi* would've said; that's what he died for. Things aren't supposed to be easy," I said knowing these words didn't console many Cubans anymore. "You're talking like an imperialist."

"Listen to you, my little *pionero*," she smiled finding it hard to believe that I knew what I was saying. "You talk and talk. Uli, can't I find *my* happiness and attempt to make things

15

easier?" She was losing her patience, and I knew she would soon say things I didn't particularly want to know.

"I love you, *Mami*," I acquiesced.

I didn't understand it. All that talk about time just baffled me more. How was time running out for her? All I could do was stand there looking out the rain-beaded window, seeing my father's memory blow like trash in the Havana wind, knowing his wife would soon be sharing her bed with that sneaky bastard from Camagüey.

"Are we ready?" she smiled, giving me her arm.

"We're ready," I mumbled, afraid to let out any tears. The deluge outside kept pouncing on the cracked walls of my aunt and uncle's house. My heart broke with every blow.

CHAPTER 2

I walked my mother down the unlit aisle between the porch and the living room of Cecilia's and Francisco's home in El Vedado. My mother, Graciela, was still complaining of the spring torrents that plagued the island on her wedding day. Her limp curls were hidden under my grandmother's white lace mantilla, and her face still appeared wet and porous from the dampness in the air, regardless of how much powder coated her face.

There were borrowed metal chairs on both sides of the makeshift aisle, each unique in its deteriorated state. I noticed a few pots on the floor to catch the storm dripping in through the dilapidated roof. No doubt Aunt Cecilia had already reminded Uncle Francisco five times to fix it the next day when the rains cleared.

"¿Qué quieres que haga, mujer?" is all he ever said when she nagged him.

"Bueno, no quiero que te hagas el bobo mañana. Yo sé que se te olvidan las cosas," my aunt would snap back.

"¡Vete por ahí, anda, y déjame en paz!" and that was the end of the argument. That was the end of all their arguments.

My grandmother's Lady of Charity, about a foot high, carrying the *Niño Jesús* on her right arm and a gold crucifix in her left hand, rested over the table set up at the end of the aisle. When I looked at the glowing icon, the look on her visage spread a little peace to me. Our Lady understood what I was going through, and that provided me a little solace.

I figured there wasn't much I could do now. There wasn't anything I could do to stop Graciela from marrying the respected Dr. Antonio Trujillo. No matter how much I tried to prove to her what a worm this man was, we continued walking down the aisle. "He'll provide," is all she'd say. In a country

17

where those were ameliorating words, there wasn't much I could do but keep my father alive in the murkiness of my memories.

Everyone at the wedding was elated. It wasn't every day a widow with a teenage son married a working doctor in Havana. I wiped my forehead with the handkerchief my mother starched for me with the water used to boil the yucca; I tried to remain presentable as everybody's eyes were on me. But the handkerchief felt like sandpaper on my skin, causing hives to blister across my forehead, making me itch all night.

I knew the guests were trying to second-guess me, trying to predict my doomsday plan before I executed it upon the unsuspecting wedding guests. Some thought I was going to light the doctor's suit on fire. Really, how immature. Or they thought that I would spike the punch with a tad of lye to make everyone sick. That wasn't such a bad idea, actually pretty ingenious. But I wouldn't have done that to my mother – use the little lye she had to make soap, I mean. God knows when we would have been able to smuggle some more.

I wished that my father appeared to her as he did to me sometimes. I wished her to feel shame for what she was doing, having her son walk her down the aisle into the arms of another man. But no such luck. As much as I prayed to *Cachita* glowing peacefully on the table, my father did not appear. I think the impermeable wall of rain prohibited him from crossing to the other side that day.

I bet you the doctor knew this and asked one of his *brujero* friends to conjure up this deluge just to keep my father's apparition from materializing. Just like the doctor to play dirty. I wondered what he offered *Changó* to ensure this downpour kept the only person my mother may have listened to from making it to the wedding; the one person I knew could have convinced her that this doctor was not the cure to her – to our – ills. Maybe he promised the ancient Yoruba god some offerings such as apples or yams, or simply a machete or piece of wood since these were easier to come by than the apples or yams.

Nestor flashed the camera he just received from some relatives in the United States, blinding my mother and me. He got on one knee, looked around the room for proper lighting, and did everything he thought a great photographer should do. All I could see were spots that moved and disappeared on their own accord, saturating the clammy air. But I continued walking down the aisle allowing the spots to guide me.

"Slow down, Uli," my mother whispered still smiling at the guests who were standing, patting their cheeks and foreheads dry.

"*Sí Señora,*" I mumbled without much fretting, trying to ignore my uncle's interpretation of what I once thought was a beautiful song. I tried to walk as fast as I could to get the whole thing over with.

Uncle Francisco continued the interlude on his guitar, closing his eyes as he sang part of the chorus *cuánto te quiero.*

I handed Graciela's trembling arm to the honorable doctor, but I couldn't look into his fiery eyes. He knew he had won. Standing there in his timeworn and yellowing white suit. Craving the beautiful bride on my arm and thinking awful thoughts. I could see this through the black beard, although it hid a major portion of his face, some say to hide the remnants of a cleft palate.

He wasn't wearing his glasses and looked unnatural. You know, like when you see somebody without his or her glasses for the first time. It's eerie! He looked like a blind man who could see. But not just what *we* could see. He looked like a preternatural creature with the ability to look right past your soul. His eyes were onyx stones that pierced my mother's blank stare; it filled her every desire. Exposing his razor-sharp, crooked teeth, Dr. Antonio Trujillo gave us both an inviting gaze like that of a beast enticing its prey to enter its lair.

My father was only a myth to him. In fact, I knew he was the one who made my mother take down my father's portrait given to her at one-of-many memorials five years after his death. It was made right before my father left for Angola, and Nestor told me that Castro himself had it in one of his eighty homes before giving it to the bereaved widow. It was the only way I could remember him, and now it was put away in our dusty attic.

Ignacio, the good doctor's second cousin on his mother's side, acted as the justice of the peace. He got a handful of cigars and a few extra grams of coffee as an expression of gratitude. It wasn't much, but the doctor wouldn't hear of having his second cousin do it for free. Although Ignacio said it would have been an honor to do the nuptials for free, the doctor wasn't going to chance his reputation as an unselfish *caballero*.

Ignacio sat smiling at the table with the statue of *Cachita* holding the Baby Jesus, waiting for Francisco's wedding ballad to end. The ecru tablecloth, a gift from my father to my mother, covered the rusty aluminum worktable Uncle Francisco kept in the back shed. The nerve of them to use this gift smuggled from a training mission in Panama.

With his sports jacket unbuttoned, revealing his white *guayabera* shirt sticking to his moist belly, Ignacio sat patiently, secretly exploring for his once-gold-plated Russian buckle that disappeared under his gut.

How he maintained this weight on a Cuban diet no one knew. In fact, some people talked about Ignacio stealing food from *Hotel La Habana Libre* where he offered his calligraphy services to whatever tourists were suckered into buying "Cuban" calligraphy. Who had ever heard of Cuban calligraphy?

There didn't seem to be a need for this type of work, but tourists were eager to spend money on anything rendered as authentically Cuban. They'd have their names or their addresses done on note cards so they could mail back home. Word had it that Ignacio did pretty well with tourists. In fact, *Hotel Inglaterra* had agreed that for only fifty percent of Ignacio's total gross sales they would set him up near their gift shop.

Nestor said that it wasn't so simple. Nothing could be simple for Nestor and me. He had to exaggerate everything so it sounded better. He claimed that when Ignacio's second wife, Mirurgia, died of complications due to a bad case of pneumonia, Ignacio stuffed her in a tub full of dry ice at his home in Regla. Some said my stepfather helped Ignacio kill Mirurgia by injecting her with the Ebola virus, but most people didn't buy it.

The story went that Ignacio was so crazed by guilt that he actually ate Mirurgia – bit by little bit. Nestor said that he heard from a very good source that Ignacio munched on his salted wife everyday for years, saving fine cuts of meat for

20

special occasions such as this one. Shaving paper-thin slices of meat like that of a good Serrano ham.

That was ridiculous, of course. For one thing, no one could get that much dry ice and salt in Cuba without the proper purchase orders!

The incessant rain drowned Ignacio's words while he wiped his forehead. It was like watching one of those old movies at El Cine Yara when the projectors broke. All we could do was watch the lips moving to unfulfilled promises on a tattered screen.

We were used to creating our own dialogue to a picture without sound, so it didn't seem to bother the guests who sat still while droplets of sweat scurried down their faces. They read the bride's and groom's lips when it came time to say each other's vows.

After Graciela and Antonio signed the necessary documents, the rain now dripping through Aunt Cecilia's kitchen, the bride and groom kissed. I was glad my father missed this. I promised myself to tell him about it later when he appeared to me. I'd lie and say it was a horrible wedding, and that *Mami* was thinking of him all throughout the ceremony. I'd protect him from this unnatural act and tell him the story the way it *should've* been.

The guitar harmonized with the drumming of the filling rain buckets that seemed to be multiplying every time I looked. People danced around the obstacle course of cauldrons that collected the never-ending rain, congratulating the bride and groom. Although the guests were drenched, they continued kissing each other and dancing as if life was sweet and equitable and all of it only a dream.

"You must be so happy!" raved Mariana, one of my mother's distant relatives whom we only saw once or twice a year – whenever there was food around or we received a care package from Miami.

"Thrilled," I answered.

"What?" Mariana asked, my voice muffled in the festivities and the clapping thunder.

"Thrilled! I just couldn't be happier!" I shouted. The music paused. Even the rain ceased for a second until everyone realized it was just I. The *guaguancó* continued.

"You're probably hungry. Go. You and Nestor serve yourselves. It's not every day we have a feast like this. Your mother married a fine man. A *provider*!" The words echoed in my ears.

Nestor grabbed my arm as he saw my ears begin to turn red as they always do when I get mad or embarrassed. He didn't want me to make a scene, not that a scene would have been a bad idea. A provider? Wasn't my father a provider? Didn't my father die for his country just like other generations of Aguileras had done since the war against the Spanish?

Whether he agreed with the politics involved or not, my father died for Cuba, for posterity. My father didn't sell out his beliefs just to get an extra gram of rice or to be called a provider. He wasn't interested in feigning an illness or anything of the sort so as not to have to fight for his country. He knew his duty to his family, to his ancestors, to everything that was Cuban.

"Ulises!" called Ignacio, stuffing his face.

"Yeah."

"Try some of this roasted pork. Enjoy it while you can!" Ignacio said spitting pieces of lacerated pig flesh on my faded tie. "Here, try the *fufú*," he mumbled, handing me a plate of the garlicky plantain mash. "Needs, more *chicharrón*," he confessed.

I pictured him eating chunks of his dead wife, Mirurgia. Nestor and I looked at each other and laughed aloud. Could it be? Then, I pictured Mirurgia's torturous countenance while being roasted limb by limb and being dressed with garlic and olive oil, porting a halo of raw onion rings while freckles of culantro, *comino*, and garlic paste filled her every sinew.

"*No, gracias, Ignacio,*" I managed to whisper through my nausea, my mouth becoming drier. "I'm kind of full. I ate a lot of cake."

"Nonsense," he insisted, slapping my back. "A growing Cuban boy saying no to *masitas de puerco? ¡Come, come! Buen provecho.*"

22

He plopped pieces of sallow pork flesh on a plate, and I felt an even stronger wave of nausea engulf me. I mimed excuse me and ran to the bathroom to hurl my life away.

The banqueters didn't seem to mind Ignacio *or* his salted dead wife, though. It seemed that if this really was Mirurgia she was scrumptious. They ate so much that half the people were sick to their stomachs, asking for the Alka-Seltzer that the neighbor's relatives had sent from Miami. But they continued stuffing their faces anyway as they didn't know when they would have a hearty meal like this again.

Making her way through those congratulating her, Graciela made it to where Nestor and I were standing, tacitly signaling to Nestor to leave us alone for a minute. She looked so relieved, so happy. I knew it was my duty not to let her know how I was feeling. I wanted her to think that I, too, was consoled by Our Lady's grace and pretended to glow as she was.

"How do I look?" Nestor asked my mother before daring to speak to Gisela, chest out and shoulders back. "I think I'm going to ask Gisela to dance," he whispered to us both, pointing to Gisela who sat in one of the metal chairs swinging her white patent leather shoes.

"You look so handsome," Graciela reassured Nestor.

Nestor had developed much faster than I had, and it incensed me how he had recently started to notice girls, sometimes talking of nothing else. His shoulders had broadened much more than mine, so we no longer traded T-shirts. His dark peach fuzz was clearly metamorphosing into a fine Cuban moustache that the girls were starting to find handsome. Even though we were the same age, people often thought Nestor was my older brother, as he looked like a much older version of me.

Comforted and smelling his breath on his hand, Nestor strutted towards Gisela who sat there pretending not to notice my cousin prancing like a wild peacock for her attention.

"*¿Cómo estás, Uli?*" my mother asked, draping me with her arms now that we were alone.

"Fine," I lied. What else was I to say? I looked into her eyes that were filled with so much hope. I had never seen such a serene look on her face.

23

Graciela took a deep breath and closed her eyes, smelling the rain. "We're going to Marina Hemingway tomorrow."

"Isn't that only for *turistas*?" I asked accusingly, knowing quite well that the only people who were allowed to vacation there were tourists with foreign currency and *jineteras* who helped the visitors pass the time. No Cubans; no *pesos*.

"Antonio knows somebody who got us two cottages. One for Antonio and me, and the other for you and Nestor. Are you surprised?" she giggled like a little girl on the morning of Three Kings Day. "Antonio wants you and Nestor to come with us!"

"Yes, I do," confirmed the doctor who materialized from behind my mother out of nowhere. His eyes glistened as he talked and held my mother from behind. His breath smelled like he had stuffed himself with mint and limes and chugged it all back with some Havana Club. It was unnatural, positively aberrant to see him hold her from behind like this. My mother laughed even louder as he surprised her.

"That'll be great! Wait until I tell Nestor," I forced myself to say and cracked a smile.

I kept fighting the urge to tell her how dispirited I was that she swapped my father's memory for this suitor's company. But I had already said enough, and she didn't seem to care how I felt. Reconciling the fact that she had completed with her duty of rearing me, there was no need for her to continue playing the role of the proud and lonely widow of a Cuban hero. As my aunt reminded me on several occasions before tonight, "Now it was time for her to move on and embrace life" – whatever that meant.

I didn't like change. Aside from all our hardships, that's one reassuring thing about Cuba; there wasn't much change in the last three or four decades. It spoiled me into believing that I would never have to adapt to new circumstances. As hungry and desperate as my comrades and I often were, it spoiled me into believing that life would remain the same for the rest of my life. There's something comforting in that. Nevertheless, new things had just begun to happen, and I suppose it was my obligation to adapt.

The satiated banqueters began to leave my aunt and uncle's house carrying plates of leftover cake, roasted pork, lentil stew (with chunks of mystery meat everyone devoured), and whatever else Ignacio and the doctor managed to get their paws on. The banqueters looked like wet dogs wagging their tails, roaming the streets of Havana futilely trying to find a safe place to bury their bones.

Many of them were talking about volunteering at the Pan-American Games. The doctor even promised those who volunteered would receive a brand new Adidas track suit just like the one Castro had been wearing for weeks while promoting these games.

Ana-Belkys even admitted that she hoped this would bring the change our country needed. As ridiculous as I thought of us Cuban socialists in Adidas sportswear, I was sort of grateful that my compatriots still exhibited the courage to hope for a better future.

My father had *not* died in vain.

CHAPTER 3

The next morning people hastened trying to repair damages from the previous night's deluge. The news briefs said everything was under control and that civil workers were on the job round the clock. It must've been Castro's famous invisible army, because I couldn't see anybody but my comrades working on their own homes. Some of our neighbors were saying that with more rain forecasted, the water would soon be going right over the *malecón*. (But if there's one thing you need to know about my comrades is that will-be's and shall-be's were really only maybe's.)

It just didn't feel right leaving that morning for Marina Hemingway with Nestor and the honeymooners. What was I to do? The plans had been made and I was not in a position to argue. One of the managers of the hotel provided us with a car, and we headed towards Jaimanitas to begin the honeymoon.

"How come we get to go to the marina?" I asked the doctor. Nobody in the car seemed to even think of what we nationals were going to do at a resort that segregated our own comrades from the rest of the world.

"Some people owe me a favor," Antonio said looking at me through the rear-view mirror, silently relishing my unhappiness. "I've got an important meeting, and they're kind enough to allow us – to invite us to stay for awhile."

"What kind of meeting?" I quickly asked.

"Uli, Antonio has been nice enough to bring you and Nestor along. Let's not ask a lot of questions. You almost sound ungrateful," Graciela interjected. The doctor put his hand over hers and smiled approvingly.

26

Nestor broke the tension. "I can't wait to go back and tell everybody I stayed at a cottage at the marina!"

"What about if you hate it?" I asked.

"Then I'll lie and say I am the luckiest *cubanito* in the world!" Nestor stated matter-of-factly.

"He won't hate it," assured my mother's husband, laughing at Nestor's retort, not taking his eyes off the muddy road. "They've got things you boys have only dreamed about! Things you've only seen in the movies!"

"Oh, I can't wait," applauded my mother, turning around to assure me that we were going to have a grand old time and that there was nothing to feel guilty about. We were about to experience things the rest of our comrades had only watched on a censored TV or movie screen.

To avoid any further probing, Antonio turned on the radio. After a lot of static and what sounded like a drunk from Bayamo singing a twangy *son*, the national radio came in loud and clear:

"...continue to be defeated. The counter-revolutionary traitors were shot this morning at dawn."

"Bang, bang!" Nestor shot at me with his index finger. He could be so immature at times. But I pretended to die in the back seat anyway after a few convulsions.

"Turn it up," I asked.

"It's just a bunch of *gusanos,*" Nestor mumbled looking at the downed power lines out the car window.

The radio announcer continued, "...which our stealthy army captured last week. Before their trial, the traitors confessed their connection with the Omega underground movement. *El Comandante* spoke just moments ago about the rumors of the growing underground organization."

The announcer paused while a recorded Fidel Castro spoke, "We will execute all individuals who continue to risk the safety of our country! Of our nation! Of our Cuba!" The recorded audience applauded with fervor. "There have been rumors that the underground group of *gusanos imperialistas* known as Omega is growing. I promise you today, as I promised you decades ago, we will die before becoming what this country

27

once was: Caribbean puppets to imperialist nations around the world!" The thundering applause lasted two whole minutes! In fact, the doctor played with the radio dial to make sure it wasn't static.

El Líder continued, "Never has our country been stronger. I promise you that the small – very small at that, a few handfuls maybe – the small cells that remain are at this very moment being detained and will be shot after their due trial!"

The radio began playing *el himno Bayamés*, and Antonio turned it off. No one said a word. Nestor was too busy staring out the window for a perfect place to pull off and pee. Having heard hundreds of speeches like these that truly meant nothing for kids our age, I too began looking out the window for a good place off the road to tell the doctor to stop so I could relieve myself. I noticed my mother grabbed her groom's knee as if asking if everything were all right.

About a half an hour later, we reached the end of Jaimanitas, the forbidden part of the island where the Marina Hemingway complex stood. Even though we had been to Santa Fe, one of the few beaches that citizens were allowed to visit, and had seen glimpses of the marina across the barbed-wire fence, I had never stepped foot on the actual Marina Hemingway. And as much as I hated to admit it, I was as excited as Nestor and my mother.

The cottages and villas of the marina looked like an oasis out of one of Hollywood's pictures. Royal palms with twinkling lights surrounded two-story cottages. The freshly painted walls and signs reminded me of the pictures my grandmother used to show me when I was little, the ones she kept under her bed with all her sewing paraphernalia.

The ivy festooning the walls of the main hall made it look like a protected castle, separate from the rest of the world. Even during the day, the sconces erupted with half-meter flames. They lit the red carpet to the entrance of the main hall. Everything was bright, too bright. Even the hibiscus looked like wax and silk. Nestor and I quickly put on our black American glasses given to us by the doctor before arriving at the marina.

We heard these glasses were like the ones Tom Cruise and other movie stars wore in the U.S.

No one spoke as we took in all this paradise. To think that this was always here. The nights when I woke up sweating, dreaming of my father. The long hot days when we reaped soybeans that would bulk up the ground beef to quadruple its yield. The nights we sat in darkness talking to shadows due to *El Comandante's* energy conservation efforts. If I had known this existed, I would have flocked here a long time ago. I mean I knew it was here, but not really. Doesn't make sense, I know.

Three men exited the main hall and greeted my stepfather who walked away so we couldn't hear what they were saying. I looked at Nestor as I didn't like the looks of this. What was he telling them? Were we going to be arrested for trespassing on a taboo piece of the island where only *turistas* were allowed? As much as I tried to get my cousin's attention, Nestor was too busy looking at the Jet Skis out in the marina and at the gluttonous displays of food by the beach.

I secretly dreamed of riding a Jet Ski, ambivalent at the thought that this was imperialist trickery. But if the rest of my comrades couldn't ride one of these, I wouldn't even consider riding one. What would my father think? What would I tell him the next time he appeared to me in my room?

All in all, it was difficult for a fourteen-year-old not to marvel at the slick, nautical lines of these crafts and wonder how it would feel to have the water thrash against the sides of the Jet Ski while still maintaining eye contact with the pink and yellow horizon.

Well, maybe I *would* try riding one. If the *Comandante* could walk around wearing Adidas suits and Pumas, then I could certainly ride a Jet Ski – just to let my comrades back home know that they weren't missing much. Yeah, I'd do it for their sake.

Antonio came back and said, "They're still preparing the cottages. Graciela, why don't you take the boys around the grounds or to the beach? They make the best piña coladas down there – real rum. Just tell the waiters to bill it to Mr. Mendelsen's account."

29

Then, the man in the seersucker suit stepped forward. His aviator glasses were elegantly propped on the bridge of his nose, his blond locks covering half the bottle-green lenses. I had seen pictures of these glasses in magazines smuggled from the U.S., but I had never seen a pair so close, never seen my own reflection off a rich, verdant pair of imperialist glasses.

"¿*Qué tal?*" he greeted in the worst Spanish I'd ever heard; it sounded like "*Kay tall.*" His white teeth smiled at all of us the same way the doctor smiled at my mother at times.

"Nice to meet you," my mother smiled back. "This is my nephew, Nestor, and my son, Ulises."

"Ah, you speak English," Mr. Mendelsen was pleased to hear.

"We've learned well in school," she attempted to say. It didn't seem like it sounded quite right because Mr. Mendelsen's expression was the same as mine when I heard him utter his two words of Spanish.

"I've got to take care of some things with Mr. Mendelsen, Graciela. Why don't you go down to the beach and have a drink," the doctor encouraged. "Go eat. I know Nestor must be starving!"

"You bet!" Nestor agreed. Everyone chuckled.

"Things are going to be much better for you and your mother," Antonio nodded to me, putting his arm around my shoulder. "Look around, have fun."

I ducked from under his grip and walked to where Nestor was standing akimbo breathing in the ocean air. Graciela just shook her head to her bridegroom as if saying *don't worry.*

Antonio and Mr. Mendelsen walked away to where the other two men stood waiting. The taciturn men just followed my stepfather and Mr. Mendelsen into the cottage after opening the door for them.

"Ready to have the best time of your lives?" my mother tempted. Nestor's face lit up filled with ideas how we could spend the next four days.

"Let's eat!" my cousin immediately said.

He led us to one of the buffet spreads surrounding the Olympic-sized pool. Beach balls with the Marina Hemingway

30

logo glided over the crystal-chlorinated water propelled by the Caribbean breeze. Children with animal-shaped life preservers splashed around their parents who attempted to steer them in one direction or another. There were inflatable alligators, swans, giraffes, and cock-eyed sea serpents that were as foreign to me as these people were to my island.

We stepped up to the first heated tray at the buffet and stared at the grilled lobster tails. None of us had ever tried these red, creepy-crawlers of the sea as food like this was reserved solely for tourists in hotels. Smelling the grilled shellfish, I knew these certainly had to be better than what we were used to eating on a daily basis. A man in a red jacket smiled at me waiting for my order. Rings of permanent sweat cuffed his underarms, but he never took off his jacket. Now that's duty!

"It's three of us," I said to him, not really knowing what I was supposed to tell him, not knowing if I was just supposed to grab one of the tails and walk away.

"That's fine, there's enough for everybody," he smiled, noticing my Cuban accent but not allowing this to affect his cordiality. "What would you like, *caballero*?" he nodded, the top of his bald red head perspiring.

"*Langosta*," I said, wondering what my neighbors who were presently draining their flooded homes would think of me at this very moment, wondering what my *compañero* serving us thought about having to call me *caballero*. Did he think I sneaked in? Or did he think I was just a good *pionero* who Castro was rewarding with a weekend pass to the marina?

My comrade took my plate, placing a colossal crimson tail on the blue and white china.

"*Gracias*," I said.

"*A la orden, caballero*," the sweaty redcoat nodded and proceeded to take Graciela's plate.

Before I had a chance to sit down and wait for my mother and Nestor, another redcoat took my plate and gave me a huge heap of Lyonese potatoes. At least that's what it said on the embossed card propped in front of the heated tray. They smelled like the best potatoes I would ever taste. Undoubtedly, Lyon was the place to go if you wanted good potatoes.

31

As I glanced down the buffet, I noticed a string of more redcoats waiting to fill plate after plate just for me. There were fancy, stenciled note cards propped in front of the rest of the heated trays just like in front of the potatoes. They read: *Caldo Gallego*, *Pollo con quimbombó*, Grilled Prawns in Plum Wine Sauce, Squid Couscous, Green Oysters, *Picadillo de Pescado*, and the list went on and on.

It was like a runaway bus. I was going to have to jump off and land wherever I land. I turned around and told my mother and my cousin that I'd get us a table and order us drinks, hoping the other waiters wouldn't shout at me or laugh for not continuing down the food line. My cousin Nestor grabbed four plates; he dared to try a little bit of everything, including the oily green oysters.

The sun worshippers strolling around with crystal flute glasses spoke French, German, Italian, and a really strange Spanish that sounded like they were singing or telling a joke. Planning next year's rendezvous in the Caribbean, they drank and ate to their hearts' content wondering why the entire world didn't decide to move here.

Nestor could imitate all their accents perfectly! My mother couldn't help but laugh as my cousin made the most whimsical faces when imitating these vacationers. He'd scrunch down his eyebrows and cross his eyes, or he'd put a pouting expression and deepen his voice. Graciela reminded him that it wasn't humorous to make fun of the way some people spoke, but his next impression of a Quebecois holding his cigarette like a 1920's silent screen star forced her to laugh along with us.

A group of calypso players set up for their next jam session. Their instruments sounded like they were throwing pennies at Coke bottles, and the sound made fun music to dance to. I believe it made the food taste better, too, because Nestor and I continued eating as they played.

A group of inebriated, red-faced Brits jumped into the conga line and raved at how much fun Cuba was and how Castro was a saint in reclaiming the island decades ago. Nestor continued making fun of their accents.

"I'm glad you came with us, Uli, Nestor," my mother said reaching over to wipe the side of my mouth.

"Me too," I answered pulling back as I was too grown up for her to wipe my mouth at the table, especially in public. Mocking me, Nestor grabbed his napkin and wiped the other side of my mouth while he batted his eyelashes. I whacked him on the back for making fun of me.

"Things are going to be so much easier for us. The worst is over, Uli."

"Is that what Antonio's talking to those Americans about?"

"What?" my mother answered nervously. She stared at me and then at Nestor who was too busy looking at two teenage Mexican girls splashing each other in the chlorinated water. Nodding her head after taking a big gulp of her third banana daiquiri, my mother laughed off the question. "You're just like your father. Thinking all the time about things that don't concern you. Are you having a good time or not?" she nudged my chin.

"Yeah, I'm glad I'm here," I hated to admit.

"Antonio is really trying hard."

I didn't respond. I just thought about what Americans could be doing on our island and why Antonio was working with them.

Nestor and I hung around the pool all day while my mother had the first facial and Swedish massage of her entire life. We forgot about the flooding homes and streets back in El Vedado. We forgot about Aunt Cecilia fighting with Uncle Francisco about finishing his chores around the house before he sat down to watch any baseball on TV. We forgot everything. Before we knew it, the day had practically ended. We still hadn't seen much of the doctor or his friends. Business, my mother assured us.

The descending sun cast hues of pink, reminding the gulls that this was a good time to stir up some food while the shore remained calm. I had never noticed the palette of our horizon back home. Not even at the voluntary work camp where the city lights were so far away had I noticed the colors of a Cuban dusk. Sipping our umbrella-donned virgin piña coladas,

33

silently praising Cuba's natural splendor, I knew this was only a vacation. I'm not sure Nestor realized this would all end for us in just a few days.

I tried not to catch even a glimpse over the barbed wire fence of my comrades leaving Santa Fe Beach. Riding three to a rusty bicycle, swerving until they caught enough speed to balance their weight, the last of the day's sun worshippers left Santa Fe while I sat sipping coconut drinks that were meant to remind tourists of Cuba, a Cuba that was clearly unknown to us who lived here every day.

My grandmother used to talk about the time when it didn't matter which direction you went, you were bound to hit a white-sand, crystal clear beach with thousands of people, natives and tourists alike, playing, drinking, and singing to badly tuned guitars. Nestor and I often thought she was exaggerating. After all, how did the government control us if they just let you walk wherever you wished?

On humid summer days, usually after we were back from the work camp, my cousin and I often took the *camello* buses to visit Santa Fe. The Marina Hemingway complex was somewhat visible from there, and we often stared at the vacation spot after a long swim or after running around when all that was left to do was sit and ponder. We would close our eyes and replenish our empty stomachs with the smells of the seasoned grills sizzling under the same scorching sun that tanned our skins, guessing what they were grilling for their auspicious guests.

The complex seemed larger than life from the other side of the fastidiously kept fence with its small hotel, villas, canals, and harbor that protected over four hundred foreign sailboats and yachts. I had told Nestor that it always looked like one of those metallic 3-D postcards or like one of those religious pictures that changes images depending from which angle you view it. To Nestor, Marina Hemingway always looked like those pictures in his dusty, unopened children's Bible of the pearly gates with velvety white clouds surrounding it.

I wondered how many of my *compañeros* lazily peered over the barbed wire fence from Santa Fe that day wondering

34

who we were on the other side peering right back at them. Did they cover and uncover one eye to see if the image of the sacred fortress changed? Did they laugh at the Mexican, Chilean, and Canadian women who paraded around in their matching two-piece bathing suits that purposely failed to hide their round bellies? I wondered if my comrades knew that there were real Cubans sitting here too, Cubans who were ready to verify that the hallowed bastion really existed once we returned to their world.

Regardless, the music, the food, the security of being anesthetized for a few days was overwhelmingly convalescing, I must admit. I didn't want to spoil it for my mother, either. She was right. She deserved a break, and it was our duty to enjoy ourselves while we could.

So this is why foreigners flocked here all-year-round. I could never figure out why *turistas* came to our island when there were so many islands around the world to choose from, islands where the natives were allowed to enjoy the same freedoms and social benefits as those who visited them. Now I knew. This was paradise. Not my paradise nor my comrades', but a tourist's paradise nevertheless.

The lifting breeze gently stroked our freshly baked faces while Nestor continued to eat the guava and cream cheese pastries the waiters brought by. I drank the rest of my virgin piña colada not wondering where my mother's husband was, not wondering where my father was, not wondering how my neighbors managed with last night's deluge. Nothing. I thought of absolutely nothing. So this was paradise.

CHAPTER 4

Although it was the first time that Nestor and I had ridden Jet Skis, the next day we raced these watercrafts, showing some Quebecois and Spaniards the "Cuban" rules we had just improvised, making the races quite exciting. A couple of German kids who followed us around all the time told us how wonderful it must be to live in Cuba. Nestor and I agreed. There was no need to go into how different our lives were outside of this part of Jaimanitas. There was no need to explain that this was as much a vacation for us as it was for them.

After lunch, we sat under the shade of the palm fronds pointing out the *jineteras* who strolled in with the VIPs. Our new friends were mesmerized by the pendulous swing of the *jineteras'* hips. The working girls seemed to have been regulars here as everyone greeted them like long-lost cousins.

Jineteras were easy to find if you had a rental car, a foreign accent, and foreign currency. Cab drivers took tourists to the *malecón*, the seawall promenade where the girls and boys usually hung around smoking cigarettes. Some of the girls and boys were as young as Nestor and me, but this didn't seem to bother the vacationing octogenarians who solicited them.

My cousin bragged about how he had been with hundreds of *jineteras*. I didn't embarrass him by telling our new friends that *jineteras* only accepted dollars or any other foreign currency and would not be caught dead sleeping with a real Cuban, unless it was their boyfriends who undoubtedly didn't know of their girlfriends' enterprising endeavors. Besides, the expressions on the other kids' faces were entertainment enough.

"And how did it feel?" asked José-María, one of the boys from Spain who spoke like my grandmother did by lisping all his z's and some c's. Never the s's though, hmm. His eyes remained wide open.

"It felt like..." Nestor sat there thinking, his right fist cradling his chin like a philosopher waiting to say something judicious.

"Weren't you scared?" asked Uwe, another of our new foreign friends, not waiting for Nestor to answer how it felt to be with a woman.

"Scared?" Nestor grimaced. "What are you, a *maricón*? It felt good. She said I did it better than some of her usual, more experienced customers. She said I was a real man and that I must come see her more often or she would just die."

The boys all patted Nestor on the back and then patted each other on the back while talking at the same time. Even though we didn't understand each other's native languages, we clearly understood how proud we were of Nestor and how lucky they were for sitting here waiting to hear the secrets of life.

Nestor sat back with his hands locked behind his head relishing the esteem.

We sat there a good portion of the day hearing Nestor's other farfetched stories, such as how he learned how to tell between real breasts and implants, how to make sure the rhythm method really worked, and how to know if a girl was faking it. It wouldn't have surprised the covey of boys if Nestor turned around and walked on water. I knew my cousin lied and exaggerated, but at that moment, I couldn't be prouder to call him my best friend.

He made an impression on the kids that they would carry with them the rest of their lives. Nestor had just made himself immortal and internationally distinguished. No doubt these kids would share these newly discovered truths with others back in Spain, Germany, Canada, and wherever else life would lead them. They would spread Nestor's gospel and make sure his message continued to be passed down from generation to generation. It was their duty as men, Nestor reminded them, to pass all this knowledge on and, most importantly, to remember to give him credit.

Before long, there would be a statue of Nestor erected in all the patriarchal capitals of the world. Men from all around would come visit his icon on their knees. A pilgrimage, just like those who go on *el Camino de Santiago*.

People thousands of years from now would have visions of Nestor. They'd gather at the side of buildings swearing the rust stains draping the skyscrapers were actually his visage. Pubescent boys would swear Nestor appeared to them in the woods or by the lake with a new message for his followers in these latter days.

With most of the day almost over, and the heat was certainly getting to all of us, our *turista* friends wondered how they could purchase some time with a *jinetera* at the hotel. Since the boys' parents hardly gave them any cash, maybe a few traveler's checks for trinkets and snacks, our foreign friends asked if there was any such thing as a group rate. They were willing to pay in any currency the *jinetera* required.

We told them that these ladies were hardcore professionals and probably wouldn't go for it unless a grownup arranged it and paid them beforehand. And with this economy, we were probably looking at paying in Japanese Yen!

"No!" the boys gesticulated, not wanting any grownups involved and certainly not having any Japanese currency.

"We just want a kiss!" Uwe said. "How much for a kiss?"

"Just a kiss?" My cousin rolled his eyes to the back of his head, "You guys are babies!"

CHAPTER 5

That night, Nestor and I sat at the open-air bar made of dried palm fronds and driftwood and we drank Roy Rogers, a good American drink that all the American boys drank, the bartender assured us. We told him we'd tip him later if he didn't make these *virgin*. He obliged.

We were bored that there wasn't much to do after the beach closed except dancing at Los Caneyes, the famous marina dance club. We tried to arrange an evening fishing trip through the marina's fishing club, but we were just put on a waiting list because reservations had to be made far in advance. Being that we weren't much in the mood to mingle with more foreigners, that fun had passed, Nestor and I just sat there with the Caribbean breeze caressing our sun-kissed shoulders.

On our own, Nestor and I decided to follow the next pretty *jinetera* up to her room. Just to see what would happen. Even though we both lied to each other about how many times we had done it, we figured if we could peek through a window, we would learn a few things – purely an educational excursion, of course.

At about midnight, my mother and the doctor thinking Nestor and I were sound asleep, the most beautiful *jinetera* in the world arrived with her sleazy *chulo*. This was strange to Nestor and me because *jineteras* were usually sent to the marina without their pimps. Since when did *chulos* deliver their goods to a foreigner at the expense of being shot? Nestor assured me that this *jinetera* was really a transvestite and that's why she was being accompanied by her bodyguard, but I ignored his observation as this lady was one of the most beautiful women I had ever seen.

It must've been a special deal, or the foreigner simply expected some kind of gallantry. Nestor finally remembered that pimps always escort their best girl to a new client, gave them a special password so that whenever the *turista* came back to the island, the hotel arranged for the girls to be delivered immediately. It made perfect sense, so I believed him.

There was something about the hips of a Cuban woman that always whet our appetites. Her figure pressed against the yellow sequin top she wore as she whispered something into her *chulo's* ear. The butterflies in my stomach began fluttering.

"I'd do it twelve times easy," Nestor boasted, watching the couple walk into Los Caneyes.

"Twelve times?" I couldn't conceal my astonishment.

"You probably don't even know what that feels like. Admit it, you've never done it," my cousin taunted.

"Yeah, I have," I lied. "But not twelve times," I replied, not knowing why he took pleasure in pretending this was natural. "You're sick, Nestor. Besides, I've known you all my life, hung out with you every day, and I know *you've* never done it."

"Oh yeah?" is all Nestor could say.

"Yeah."

After a few seconds of awkward silence, and watching the working girl walk away from our view, I asked, "Why does she have so many bags?"

"Toys."

"Toys?"

"Yeah," Nestor insisted. "She's got all sorts of stuff in those bags. How's she supposed to know what kind of kinky things her client is into? Especially those Germans! Didn't you hear Uwe?"

We decided that maybe going into the club wasn't such a bad idea, if only to go back to our friends the next day and tell them how much fun we had while they were tucked in bed. We'd exaggerate, of course, and tell them we wined and dined the finest women on the island and that it was too bad they were so busy wasting their vacation sleeping.

40

A *guaguancó* greeted us way before we even got a glimpse of the famous Los Caneyes dance club. Hearing unfiltered Cuban music like this made our bodies resonate. Laughter and clinking glasses soon joined the beat of a cha cha cha that usurped the *guaguancó*, our hips swaying ever so slightly to the music.

"They're not going to let us in," I whispered to my cousin. "I don't care who my stepfather is."

"Leave it all up to me," Nestor winked.

"Oh, God, don't embarrass me. *Por favor.*"

"When have I ever..." my cousin began to say, but he knew I was ready with a plethora of examples. We both laughed without saying another word.

To my amazement, we were greeted cordially at the door by a leather-skinned man whose smile was so wide we could see the metalwork on his molars.

"*Bienvenidos a Los Caneyes, jóvenes*" he said, lowering his glance as if we were royalty. Did he not notice we were not old enough?

"Hope you and the good doctor are having a good vacation."

"Ah, yes, *compañero,*" I greeted back, surprised he knew who we were. My cousin jabbed my ribcage reminding me that this type of vernacular would probably not be tolerated here. He was probably right. Tourists would probably find it distasteful to hear me calling my comrade a comrade. No need to remind them or us, for that matter, where we truly were.

The club was the most beautiful spectacle I had ever visited in my life. The people, too. Electric fans made of palm fronds, which were really plastic but looked as real as any palm frond I had ever seen, kept the dancers and drinkers cool. The plastic fronds contained red lights on the edges which made me dizzy when I tried to follow just one of the blades around and around to try and see how these lights were arranged.

There was a dance floor in the very center of the club with actual lights built into its surface. I don't know how they did it, but the lights blinked and sizzled along with the beat of

41

the music. Perhaps this was a way to aid those tourists who couldn't keep their hips gyrating to the 2:3 Cuban beat.

Above the dance floor, multi-colored lights gyrated faster and faster like helicopter propellers. Hoisted on miniature cranes, lights lowered and flew around as the music grew faster and faster. Blue sirens on the tip of black cones came down and made the dance floor and everyone on it look like they were covered in sapphires. There must've been a million lights, including the strobes, pulsating just seconds apart and keeping to the rhythm of the music.

There were two wall-length bars attached to each other to form an L. It was remarkable to me that my comrades tending bar could keep up with what appeared to be thousands of different bottles behind them. They almost reached for these bottles without even looking. Must've taken a lot of training and memorization.

The wall to the left of where we entered was a titanic fish tank with fishes of every color, every hue. There were coquettish parrotfish, whimsical clown fish, magisterial angelfish, and several tiny fish that seemed to have neon lights for blood. Seahorses galloped through the water, of which a few were pregnant. Nestor told me that the pregnant seahorses were actually the males. I just nodded knowing this was one of Nestor's most outlandish tales.

Tables that sat two to six surrounded the sides of the dance floor opposite the bars. I saw the parents of our newly made friends smoking Havanas and drinking out of balloon-shaped glasses. Like an organized ant trail, the waiters bounced off each other to make it to their assigned tables, not allowing any glasses to go empty or any woman, married or not, to go thirty seconds without being complimented.

The *jinetera* Nestor and I saw come into the club walked with her boss through the tables. Every gentleman stood, erecting his cigar away from the lady's face, to greet the *jinetera* while their wives looked down or held on to their husband's sleeves to assure themselves their husbands wouldn't stray.

Why was everyone greeting the *jinetera* that way? Was she that famous that everyone knew her? Nestor insisted that her boss was marketing the goods; made sense to me. Then, she went back around the bars and through a swinging door placarded *No Pasar. Sólo Empleados de Los Caneyes.*

"What time is the show?" an Argentine man asked me.

"What show?" I asked back.

"What show?" The Argentine asked me in shock. "Why, Zyrena, of course!"

"Zyrena?" My voice was drowned by the beating drums of the Cuban *son*.

The Argentine pointed to a picture next to the fish tank of the girl Nestor and I thought was a prostitute. ZYRENA in silver glitter letters crowned the picture frame.

"*No sé*," I whispered and walked toward the picture as if in a trance.

"Where you going?" my cousin asked, yanking my arm.

"Look," I pointed. "She's not a *jinetera*. She's some sort of famous person. Zyrena," I said, letting her name suck the wind out of me as I said it. "Zyrena," I repeated.

"No shit!"

"No shit," I nodded.

The music ended with three perfect *Tan! Tan! Tan!* as dancers and drinkers scurried to their tables, some having to stay standing and some even taking seats on the floor in front of the dance floor.

"Ladies and Gentlemen!" a voice reverberated in the speakers. "*Mesdames et Messieurs*, Los Caneyes is proud to present the one...the only...the voluptuous...Zyrena!"

The crowd applauded with fervor, drowning out the beginning of Zyrena's *bolero*.

From behind a curtain made of what appeared to be lighted icicle strands on the far end of the dance floor, entered Zyrena, her hair and lashes much longer and fuller than what I remembered her walking in with.

Her lashes were highlighted with tiny diamond-like studs, accenting her azure eyes. She nodded in appreciation and began her siren song, captivating everyone in the room. Making sure the length of her garnet, sequined dress didn't cause her to trip or get stuck in one of her garnet, sequined heels, Zyrena gently moved her hips and kicked her legs forward.

Nestor and I paved our way into the crowd and closer to the dance floor to witness the Cuban diva croon. Zyrena walked around the tables, demurely flicking her long fingernails on some of the gentlemen's chins who were blessed enough to sit up close.

Everyone felt she was singing to them and only them. She made eye contact even with the waiters who, regardless of the fact that several tourists' cups went empty, stood in place not daring to move a muscle, lest they miss Zyrena's every nuanced movement.

At one point, she even looked right at me, right into my eyes, right into my very soul. Her piercing stare made me gulp and left me wanting for more. *Look this way*, I prayed. *Just one more time.*

Nestor, of course, claimed the glance was meant for him, but I knew she was looking at me as she mouthed *te amo*, only then to close her studded-lined eyes to emphasize how much she meant those lyrics.

We moved closer to the bar near the swinging door of what must've been her dressing room. If nothing else, maybe we could exchange glances one more time before she exited the dance floor.

The bartender poured us two Cuba Libres at Nestor's request, which I couldn't stomach. Nestor said we weren't used to rum, but it was our duty to start learning how to drink it. I couldn't imagine ever liking the stuff. He told me it was made of sugarcane, but it must've been diet sugarcane, because there was nothing sweet about the taste of it.

The audience applauded approvingly, some men even whistling the way Nestor tried to show me once, with two fingers under my tongue. But none of this fazed the mesmerizing singer. She continued to move from section to section, assuring that even the quiet spectators, those like me who couldn't whistle or were too shy to shout out in front of their wives, received their fair share.

Nestor, on his third Cuba Libre, began whistling and yelling, *"¡Bella!"* I was mortified, but it seemed to catch her attention, consciously or subconsciously. Zyrena slithered her way to where my cousin and I leaned on the bar and winked at Nestor. This only egged on his catcalling, *"¡Bella, mamita!"*

As I looked down to the floor, embarrassed that everyone's eyes must certainly be on us, I felt a pinch on my cheek and someone tousle my hair. Thinking it was Nestor, teasing me for not being Zyrena's object of affection for those two seconds, I looked up only to see Zyrena's crystal blue eyes peer right into mine. She smiled as she kept singing her bolero, and the audience applauded fiercely at the physical contact the seductive singer initiated with such a young boy.

I breathed. That's all I could do was breathe. The smell of Zyrena's ambrosial perfume, mixed with the softness of her velvety voice, entered my pores, my eyes, my ears, until I was practically sated with her tenderness.

For a few seconds, which felt longer than any other sensorial experience I have ever had, I was full of Zyrena, full of her words, her essence, even her fears and loathes. For those few seconds, she gave herself to me, completely and unabashedly. The rum, which I couldn't ingest before, was ameliorating and the necessary medicine for an experience like that.

After a few songs, the audience crying *"Encore! Encore!"* she exited past us, without even acknowledging our earlier exchange. My heart dropped, and Nestor insisted that we follow her into the dressing room.

Soon after she disappeared into her dressing room, Zyrena came back onto the dance floor in a red leotard with red peacock feathers as a skirt. Four male dancers, who were as graceful and feminine as she was, grabbed hold of her arms as she kicked her feet. The lights pulsed to a fast Brazilian tune, hiding the sweat she inconspicuously wiped off her brow.

The dancers kept up with Zyrena, but they certainly did not upstage her presence as she perfectly, without an accent, sang in Portuguese.

I decided the evening was over. I only wished to go to sleep while I could still smell her, while I could still feel the magic and reality of the mellifluous illusion that had taken place.

"Don't be such a chicken!" my cousin drawled, his breath reeking of one-too-many Cuba Libres. "Let's wait for her."

"I'm tired," I sluggishly whispered, my head spinning.

We made it through the waiters, dancers, and light show which ensued after Zyrena's performance and left Los Caneyes. The night was cooler than I expected. I looked up at the stars which twinkled unaware of my experience, unaware of the magnificence that was Zyrena's performance.

I couldn't understand how everything continued, how the world just didn't stop on its axis and dart us all out into space. After what I experienced in that two-second exchange, I hated the universe for continuing to exist without acknowledging my pain of knowing I'd probably never see my new love again. But the palm fronds continued waving gallantly in the breeze; the moon continued shining on our island.

"¡No quiero!" I heard a woman's voice yell.

Then, Zyrena's manager in his sharkskin suit pushed Nestor and me out of their way, Zyrena being dragged behind. The show was over, and she was being dragged out of Los Caneyes.

"I already told you, it'll only take a minute," the man insisted, his voice raspy as if he'd smoked several cartons of unfiltered cigarettes every day of his life.

"¡Oye, oye, tranquilo!" Nestor yelled, confronting Zyrena's manager, hiccupping as he waited to get punched in the face.

The man, not acknowledging Nestor's drunken words, continued leading Zyrena into one of the cottages.

"Nestor, she doesn't want to go with him! We gotta do something!"

"Ah, let her go. Let's go for a swim," he hiccupped again.

46

"Nestor, c'mon! We gotta save her," I pleaded. Just when I thought I'd never see her again, here I had a chance to save her and win her love.

We decided to wait and see if we heard any screams or any signs of struggling. We'd wait outside the cottage or outside her door to try to hear something. Nestor decided that we must wait for the lights to be turned on in the cottage and then follow them up.

This was the same cottage where the doctor had had the meeting with Mr. Mendelsen. There were windows on the leeward side, and as expected, a light flickered on. Nestor and I climbed to the balcony when the lights immediately dimmed. We could see their shadows, but there seemed to be three people in the room. Zyrena's manager mumbled something to whoever was sitting in a leather executive's chair. We were about to jump out of our skins with anticipation.

I prayed that Zyrena wasn't going to be made to do anything she wasn't willing to do. I'd have to jump in through the window for sure! My princess needed saving, and I was ready to risk my life for her.

As our eyes focused in the room, I noticed they were not in a bedroom but in an office with leather chairs, an antique mahogany desk, and Afro-Cuban bric-a-brac peppered everywhere, making it look like someone just threw them anywhere, thoughtlessly, but you know it took someone hours to come up with such a "natural" look.

The office looked like a picture in those Ethan Allen magazines our relatives sent us from Miami every so often to show us how they were remodeling their homes in colonial Caribbean style.

The Cuban man kept his dark sunglasses on as he talked to the man in the chair. We couldn't see the man's face, but my cousin and I knew he was American; we deduced this from his lazy drawl.

"We were right all along," my cousin said, hiccupping three times in a row as if he were about to throw up. Hardly able to catch his breath, "She is a *jinetera*."

47

"Shh," I nudged him. I wasn't in the mood for more theories. My head was already pounding.

Nothing was really happening, but from the way Zyrena took a long drag from her cigarette, it was clear that the tension in the room was palpable.

The Cuban man took out a manila envelope from his shark-skin jacket. Nestor said that all foreigners had to sign a contract before using any of the *jineteras*; it was just a precaution against disease, breaches of contract, no refunds, etc. I didn't believe this. Nestor wasn't as good as I was at interpreting people's expressions.

We once took a test at school that let you and your teachers know what type of person you were. I scored highest in class in the empathic realm. My teacher said that would get me in a lot of trouble one day.

Zyrena's greasy friend solemnly threw the envelope on the mahogany desk as if saying beat this hand. Wiping his face with a black silk handkerchief that looked like it had never been used before, the Cuban man kept his eyes on the American.

Zyrena just stood there, lighting another Marlboro. Either the American already knew what was in the envelope, or he was bluffing that he didn't care. Nonetheless, his calm American accent proved that he had something up his sleeve.

Then the leather chair swiveled and the American got up. It was Mr. Mendelsen! He stood there smoking a Havana my stepfather brought him earlier. He rolled it through his fingers just staring at the couple who, by the looks of the *yanqui's* flushing cheeks, were obviously offending him.

"When are they gonna do it?" Nestor was growing impatient.

"Shh," I held my hand to his mouth. "Can't you see that something else is happening? That's not a sex contract. The guy is blackmailing Mr. Mendelsen."

"Mr. Mendelsen?" Nestor squinted.

"Yes. Those are probably pictures of Mr. Mendelsen doing something bad, probably with another woman. Mr. Mendelsen has a wedding ring. Need I say more?"

48

"You don't know anything, Uli," whispered Nestor, envious that I had deduced this from the clues before us and not from his theories. "American wives aren't like Cuban wives. American women don't care if their husbands find the company of other ladies."

"You're so full of crap, Nestor."

"Well, that's what I heard!"

"Shh!!!"

Mr. Mendelsen calmly reached in his tanned, suede jacket that looked too warm to be worn in the tropics. I was right. Mr. Mendelsen was going to have to pay for the pictures the Cuban man brought. Zyrena smiled, taking a hard drag of relief from her second cigarette. Her greasy-haired boss in the silver suit was relieved as well, but he still held onto his black handkerchief tightly as if it had the power to protect him from anything that could go awry.

Without a moment's hesitation, his cheeks ever flushed, Mr. Mendelsen gently took out a .22 caliber, which looked more like a toy than a real firearm, and he shot the blackmailer with perfect aim. The Cuban man lunged back, kicking the desk with his boots making the pictures fly everywhere. Some pictures even hit the window where Nestor and I crouched. Zyrena screamed, holding her head in disbelief, her large-loop earrings whipping her cheeks.

Two of the black and white glossies fell right below our view. They showed a group of men around an Omega anti-revolution flag. It was all too quick, but I saw my mother's new husband shaking hands with Mr. Mendelsen in one photograph and a group of men sitting around a map with the heading *Mapa Político de la Provincia de Oriente* in another. They were clearly plotting strategies of some sort.

Nestor grabbed my arm, motioning me to jump over the balcony and back to our room. Shocked at the events I just witnessed, however, I was glued to the window. Through this murderer's kindness, Nestor and I were guests at the marina. My gut feeling was right. We should have never come here. This wasn't a place for Cubans.

49

I looked up and Mr. Mendelsen grabbed Zyrena, cupping her mouth with his free hand. The *yanqui* took the gun and rubbed it against her wide Cuban hips and thighs. Adrenaline rushing through her body, the singer's eyes remained wide open. She coughed as he blew rings of smoke in her face.

Pleading with Mr. Mendelsen, feeling the cold .22 move up her thighs, she sobbed quietly. Her cries were useless, though, as Mr. Mendelsen was going to enjoy himself. It was like watching a mad scientist torture his lab rat just before putting it to death.

I couldn't believe Antonio had anything to do with this. What were the Omega pictures about? Was the good doctor that much of a snake to want to destroy his own country?

Biting Zyrena's neck as if draining her of her vital fluids, Zyrena flinched. Mr. Mendelsen feeling Zyrena jump back stopped for a brief second, assessed the situation, then gently kissed her on the nape of her neck. He pressed against her, spooning Zyrena ever so slowly, letting her feel his excitement. Americans were cool-headed, no question!

The *yanqui* raised the gun to Zyrena's head while her eyes remained closed. Her lips quickly began singing softly *Ave María*. I'm sure she prayed that her beautiful voice would mesmerize Mr. Mendelsen like it did the rest of us at Los Caneyes.

She continued singing and crying, grabbing the medal of Our Lady around her neck. Zyrena prayed this man would just fall in love with her voice and let her go. But her prayers remained ignored, and Mr. Mendelsen shot her in the back of the head. A quick snap and she lay lifeless on the desk.

Her glassy eyes, like two marbles reflecting nothing but the outside moonlight, stared at me through the window. But she didn't stare at me the way she did when singing her *bolero*. She just looked right through me, right past my very being. Fear remained frozen on her visage forevermore.

The lights went on and two other men came in, one yawning as if he was born doing this kind of chore.

Nestor had had enough and almost jerked my arm out of its socket. My cousin, now partly sober, hurdled over the

50

balcony, not caring we were up two stories. I hurried after him, knocking down an empty kerosene can in the process. Shit, I thought. I'm dead. I prayed to the *virgencita* to protect me.

Instead of thinking of poor Zyrena's soul, I just swore to Our Lady that I would go back to Fortuna's and drink chicken's blood if I got through this alive.

Landing on the soft grass, I crawled away from the window, ignoring the jolting pain in my ankles. Gasping and white as a ghost, Nestor just sat there outside the cottage.

"What do we do?" I asked. Nestor was speechless for the first time in his life. "We can't just sit here. They might've heard us!"

Nestor and I heard the roar of the waves at the end of the small path behind the cottages where the Chinese government was working with Cuba to build more villas. We looked at each other acknowledging that the path through the half-constructed villas leading to the beach was the only fathomable route of escape. I figured I'd go back for Zyrena later.

Making a run for it, we heard the front door of Mr. Mendelsen's cottage open. We dove in the water, scratching our foreheads with the bottom of the shallow shore. We didn't know where to go, so we just swam in the vastness as far as our arms and tightening lungs were willing to take us.

Jumping out of the water like a dolphin at one of the aquarium shows, gasping for air, I asked, "Do you think they saw us?" I hoped Nestor would reassure me that they didn't.

"I don't think so. We'd be dead," answered my cousin, tilting his head back while he cleared his sinuses in the black sea.

"Who were those other guys?" My cousin asked, still trying to express water from every orifice of his body.

"I don't know; *cleaners*, maybe."

I heard the word used in a gangster movie at El Cine Yara once, and Nestor and I used the word for months until it just flowed naturally into conversation. It had such a purifying ring to it. *Cleaners*. These people came in and cleaned the bad guys' mess so when the police showed up, everything was spotless. Gangster movies always romanticized these people as lonely but loyal workers who did a thankless job that nobody else wanted to do. Well, if these guys were cleaners, there was nothing romantic or heroic about them.

"Did you see the pictures?" I asked my cousin, my heart still beating as I paddled my feet to stay afloat in the tenebrous sea.

"What pictures? I was just trying not to throw up!"

We sank our heads as we saw the men leave Mr. Mendelsen's cottage. With our eyes barely above water, we looked like two crocodiles peering at the shore, two very apprehensive crocs staring at our territory being trespassed.

Mr. Mendelsen guided the other two men out of the cottage, his trepidation visible even from a quarter kilometer away. He peered into the night with the same timorous expression to which I awoke every night when dreaming of my late father.

The men dragged the bodies to a Lincoln Town car that waited obediently by the door. Simple. Cool. Clean. The *yanquis* looked around the cottage and past the villas under construction. Had they lost something? It must've not been very important as they all jumped in the black car and sped off. No one heard a thing. *Cachita* had deafened their ears to my clumsiness on the balcony.

We swam back to the beach, not realizing the time of morning. The tide groggily ebbed and flowed, leaving minuscule pools where our toes found haven.

"We can't say anything, Nestor," I warned my cousin. "Not even to my mom or my stepfather."

"We should tell Antonio," Nestor disagreed, lying back on the sand, his toes still digging into the shore.

"What?" I panicked, thinking of the picture of Mr. Mendelsen and Antonio shaking hands. "We can't!"

"Mr. Mendelsen killed those people. Your stepfather should know who he's dealing with."

"Maybe he already knows!" I said, resisting the urge to tell Nestor what I saw in the photographs.

Incredulously, "You think so?"

"Well, we don't know. And if he *does* know, then we're dead for sure." It was obvious Nestor didn't see the pictures. I decided that it was better that my cousin knew as little as possible. He had a big mouth. And this time it could get us killed.

The Marina Hemingway was asleep with its gas torches lit like candles on a birthday cake. All was quiet and serene as if all that had occurred was a dream or a movie Nestor and I had sneaked into without paying. The royal palms swayed methodically like a pendulum counting down the hours before sunrise. Nestor stared at the stars that seemed oblivious to our panic, patting the shore as if kneading bread.

"You're right," my cousin interrupted. "There's no way to know whose side Antonio's on. We better stay quiet."

I sighed with relief.

"But it's our duty," Nestor insisted, not happy about having to stay quiet. "They're the ones *El Comandante* is looking for. They must be the ones we heard about on the radio. Maybe there's even a reward! You're always talking about duty…"

I let his voice just drift past my ears like the cool ocean breeze that swept our bodies. I was no longer sure what our duty was. Before this trip I would've agreed with Nestor and called the authorities, regardless of the consequences. I knew my father would have done the same. But I was horrified at the events that would ensue if we spoke against Antonio and his North American friends. What would happen to my mother?

Thoughts swirled in my head as I looked up at the heavens that blinked with undiscriminating beauty. We lay on our backs feeling the shore ebb and flow under our shoulder blades. Afraid to return to our room, we fell asleep in the darkness.

"Uli," I heard my father whisper as I dreamed that I was in my own room in El Vedado. "Ulises."

"*Papi*, is that you?" I squinted. "Where are you? I can't see you."

"I'm over here," I heard him beckon as the waves crashed on the rocks that safeguarded this part of Jaimanitas.

My father called from the impenetrable blackness. Restraining the urge to sweep me up in his arms, the ghost stood still. He looked different, not like the father who had appeared to me so many times before. Gliding over the breakers, he stood in his army fatigues, a grave look on his visage.

"It's me, *Papi*," I whispered.

"You shouldn't be here," the apparition stated firmly.

"I know, but *Mami* wanted us to come. I just wanted to make her happy."

My father smiled, but it wasn't a smile acknowledging my generosity of spirit. It was almost a smile in response to something someone invisible whispered in his ear. What was he trying to tell me?

"Are we in danger? What's going on?" I asked, eager to feel secure.

"Play it smart, Uli. You are getting in over your head. These are not matters to be witnessed by a boy your age. Go back home. Stay there and pretend none of this occurred," he forewarned.

"Does *Mami* know?" I asked, ignoring his plea for me to forget the events that had transpired.

But my father insisted, "Go back home and pretend none of this happened. Make sure Nestor tells no one of what he saw."

"I'll try."

"You have to do better than try," he declared lifting his arms as if trying not to come too close to the imperialist-friendly shore of the Marina Hemingway. Like a bird trying to land carefully on a pier, my father continued pushing against the wind to avoid contact and maintain lift.

Lightning shattered the black sky, the darkness illuminating his sallow skin. There was no vitality in his face, no vitality in his voice. As the stormy sky set the horizon ablaze, the bewilderment in his appearance was quite evident.

The air grew still, and it became hard to breathe. I gasped in my sleep wishing I could open my eyes. Paralyzed in the sand, I attempted to move at least one muscle to jar myself awake and catch the specter in full glory. But I remained frozen in place.

My father, Ulises, gesticulated over the barbed-wire fence to the other part of the beach, the eroding Santa Fe shore where our comrades pretended to vacation whenever they could manage time to visit their native beach, ignoring the broken glass, bottle caps, and abandoned sandcastles.

He couldn't speak to me while I was indulging on this part of the island. That became obvious to me. I managed to understand what he was gesticulating, all the time trying to read his lips; it was a warning to get out. There were simply no words to further convey the ghost's angst at my remaining on this part of the island.

The thunder drummed like a bongo through the evening, as if *Changó* himself roared, calling my father's spirit back to rest. The waves slapped the rocks, not allowing me to hear what my father was saying as he was aspirated by the stars back through space. His outstretched hand reached for me, but I still couldn't move. Paralyzed with fear, I felt the wet sand on the small of my back. With a final explosion on the pier, the vision of my father vanished.

"¡Papi!" I awoke, looking around at the howling heavens, my eyes full of sticky brine. The foot of the pier laid smoking from a lightning bolt that dragged Nestor and me back to reality.

"What happened?" Nestor yawned, his shocked hair stiff from the salty water.

"My...nothing," I said, not wanting my cousin to make fun of my father's visit.

"Where are we?" he continued yawning, the palm of his hands rubbing his eyes like two windshield wipers. "Oh, my head," he complained as he turned away from me and threw up the rest of last night's rum.

"We fell asleep on the beach. You OK?" I asked.

He nodded.

We headed to our rooms as the cumulous clouds, which hid the ascending sun, gathered over the marina. Another storm was approaching our island; another dawn deluge would descend upon our people.

No one noticed sleepy-eyed Nestor and me surreptitiously sneaking back to our room. The Marina Hemingway employees scurried to cover the grills and musical

55

instruments that lay dormant awaiting another day's flock of *turistas*. Our *compañeros* in red coats looked like angry ants trying to guard their sandy home, which would probably wash away regardless of their diminutive efforts. The thunder and lightning came together almost without a pause. It was time to take shelter.

CHAPTER 6

Nestor and I did not discuss what occurred the night before. Taking the ghost's advice, I tried to forget what my cousin and I witnessed. But the image of Zyrena giving up her spirit in Mr. Mendelsen's icy arms continued playing in my head. How was I going to react when Mr. Mendelsen and my stepfather talked to us? It was going to be a difficult task, but I had to act like I knew nothing.

As soon as Nestor and I dove onto our beds, trying to catch whatever siesta was possible, a rapid knock on the door set our hearts pumping with dread. My cousin looked at me with wide eyes, telepathically expressing his well-developed paranoia.

"Uli. Nestor. Open this door!" Antonio demanded.

I was certain this was it. I hadn't heeded my father's warning in time. Instead, I lay there waiting to be accused of witnessing a clandestine meeting by one of the members of the now infamous underground movement that furiously festooned our island like rapidly asphyxiating kudzu.

"Uli! Nestor! Get up and open the door!"

I slid the chain off the door wondering if Nestor and I would end up like our two comrades we saw, giving up our spirits to an imperialist and subservient demon.

The doctor barged into the room, a bloodless face staring at us both. It was evident that he had not slept all night. His crinkled suit and sweaty, sickly semblance alarmed Nestor and me who were not used to seeing the doctor in such an unfastidious state.

"What's wrong?" Nestor asked from his bed, trying to appear as unruffled as possible.

57

Ignoring my cousin's query, and the smell of rum that my cousin and I brought back with us, looking straight into my eyes as if trying to hypnotize me but realizing he was too weak to attempt this ritual of manipulation, Antonio blurted, "Your mother's packing. It's necessary for us to leave the marina immediately. Get your things ready and meet us by the car in ten minutes."

"All right, calm down. Did something happen?" I ventured to ask, hoping he wouldn't shoot me where I stood, acting as if all we experienced last night was only a dream.

"You've got ten minutes! *¡Diez minutos!*" he gesticulated pushing both his palms close to my face as if miming someone stuck behind a confining cage. He scurried out of the room and was out of sight in seconds.

"I'm not going with him!" Nestor gulped.

"We have no choice. Get me my bag. Just throw everything in and we'll sort it out at my house."

"Uli, he knows! Isn't it obvious that he's scared shitless? I'm staying right here at the marina. Maybe they'll give me a job here or something. Maybe I'll never have to go back."

"You sound like these *turistas*. You know we can't stay. Grow up! We gotta go and forget this holiday ever happened."

I knew, though, that it was going to be difficult to give up the crystal clear cascades of the marina that draped us with amelioration, although that security meant indulging in capitalist gluttony; it was going to be difficult to return to the slate-colored shadows of political puppetry after experiencing the overwhelming reality that the rest of the world didn't live like we did, didn't covet like we did, didn't cling to make-believe distortions of physical existence the way Cubans did.

"Look, I'd love to stay too, but we've got to go back," I tried consoling Nestor.

"Yeah, I know – it's our duty!" he mocked.

"I spoke to my father yesterday and..."

"There you go again, Uli. Keep talking to *Tio Ulises* and shadows. You know what they're going to do to you? Put you away for good. They're going to stick you in that *manicomio* in

58

Matanzas. The one where they take out a chunk of your brain and you live like a zombie for the rest of your life."

"My father is not a shadow," I rebuked Nestor's enlightenment. "He told me that we need to leave Jaimanitas immediately or...or something's going to happen."

"What's going to happen, Uli?"

"Did you forget what we saw last night? I know you couldn't have forgotten what we witnessed," I charged.

"Things like that happen every day in this world."

"Not our world."

"Look, there were many people on this part of the island last night. What happened will not affect any of their lives one bit, including mine. I'm not even too sure what *did* happen. We were drunk and..." Nestor paused.

"We've gotta go home. That's all there is to it."

"The minute we go back, everyone's going to treat us differently for being here. They're going to talk crap behind our backs."

"It's too late to feel guilty now," I said. "We'll just tell them we were at Santa Fe Beach with my mother and Antonio for their honeymoon."

My cousin escaped to the bathroom as I was trying to convince him to continue packing. I heard him throwing up, and I wished I could have done the same.

"Look, I'm leaving," I stated loudly into the bathroom. "You know they're not going to let you stay. You're Cuban, *compañero*. You don't belong here," I tried to convince both him and myself. "Our place is with our comrades over that barbed-wire fence, no matter how dreary you perceive it now."

Coming out of the bathroom, as pale as my stepfather, "All right!" Nestor exclaimed, glaring at me as if I were the one taking away his brightly-lit, newfound nirvana. But he knew that being Cuban meant the government would not allow him to stay anywhere near tourists. Our compatriots who served us lunch and dinner by the pool in their red coats must've done major favors to higher-ups in order to be given the privilege to serve the foreign elite who visited Marina Hemingway every year.

59

Clothes were still strewn everywhere. Socks went into our bags without their counterparts; postcards and souvenir drink umbrellas were overlooked and remained on the writing desk, rendering no proof to our friends that we were actually here, providing no guilt once our eyes and our minds became accustomed to the wattage of our former reality.

"Ready?" I asked, quickly scanning the room for any important articles we might need back home.

"I guess," my cousin stated grabbing extra bars of soap; these would prove valuable for bartering back home.

We met my mother and stepfather downstairs by the gates. The car was already running and Graciela peeped over her new sunglasses cradled on the bridge of her exfoliated nose. Her colossal straw hat hid her face as if she were trying to leave the complex without anyone noticing.

"¿Mami?" I asked, hoping she would look at me with some sort of message in her eyes.

"Vámonos," is all she muttered, helping Nestor and me with the bags the doctor hadn't already tossed into the trunk of the borrowed car.

Nestor and I jumped into the back seat as Antonio peeled off, leaving a cloud of smoke where the gates proudly protected the foreigners' fortress. Graciela grabbed his hand as the doctor made a quick turn onto the road that led away from Jaimanitas, away from the legendary Marina Hemingway.

Something was definitely wrong. Their fright was making me more and more concerned until the thunderous blast behind our car deafened my ears. With the explosion, Antonio swerved off the road almost hitting a row of royal palms. Nestor and I instinctively dove to the floor, our faces pasted to the back-seat floor mats.

Slowly gathering courage, Nestor and I looked up, trying to see past the cloud of dust. Above the overshadowing mist, a mushroom cloud of orange then gray hues evaporated into the atmosphere. The complex had been attacked by the Omega underground! But why? Bombing your own place of business seemed compulsive, irrational, and definitely un-American.

60

The doctor sped up looking at the blaze through the befogged rear-view mirror. My mother held his hand without turning around. She couldn't witness the raining of brimstone and fire that befell on the marina.

How unnatural it was for no one to say a word. I couldn't even count on my mother's innate talent to explain the obvious. The car simply continued to speed down the unpaved roads; no one uttered a word as if the show of lights and destruction were only a dream. Perhaps the marina wasn't really there. Perhaps the explosion didn't really occur. Perhaps this was all simply a dream.

CHAPTER 7

The rains continued in Havana. This weather was going to interfere with all the construction that needed to be erected for the upcoming Pan-American Games. People were worried that news teams would start arriving without the sets being built that would portray Havana as a modern Caribbean city. They didn't want the beautifully etched Havana we knew to be shown on television.

The weather was also going to make our morning bus trip to the compulsory work camp, *el trabajo voluntario* in Tarará, a wet and muddy experience. *El Comandante* promised that the rains would soon stop; how he knew what weather we would be having was beyond me. But, my comrades reminded Nestor and me that *El Líder* knew everything – then they just laughed.

The radio continued to predict that the Omega underground movement would soon be exterminated from our island. Fervor in the radio announcer's voice helped us believe that this insurrection would soon be over. Nothing for us to worry about assured the doctor. Still, no mention of the explosion we witnessed during my mother's honeymoon.

It was almost as if the honeymoon did not occur. It was like waking up in my bed after speaking with my father's ghost, not really knowing where I was, what I was doing, nor if I truly was speaking with someone or just shadows in my room. I tried paying more attention to what the doctor was doing, but he was certainly cunning. He must've done most of his wheeling-and-dealing from his office. He'd get some late phone calls at home, but they were always quick and never conducted above a whisper.

Neither my mother nor Nestor ever mentioned the incident. I knew the doctor wouldn't discuss it as he was somehow connected to this subservience, and probably many other clandestine cases, and wouldn't dare bring it up. It was quite easy for everyone, except me, to pretend that nothing had occurred.

Nestor agreed to stay over at my house since we were going to the camp in Tarará the following day. Part of Tarará, about nineteen kilometers east of the center of Havana, in a municipality known as Habana del Este, was a gated community with mostly foreigners, foreigners who were allowed to visit the pristine beaches of Santa Maria del Mar and Guanabo.

Many Ukrainians, especially those with babies, came to Tarará after Chernobyl to recover from the fallout and for continued medical care. Most of them never left our island and remained living here, speaking the most beautiful Spanish with a Ukrainian accent.

The only time we Cubans really visited Tarará was not to visit the gated community or its beaches, but rather it was to work in the fields just outside of the municipality like all other *pioneros* our age did on a rotating basis.

We wondered whether we'd be digging up malanga or yucca or if we'd just be tilling soil. It was hard to say since there was always a new Agricultural Minister trying to implement his or her theories that they'd developed over the years in some dimly lit laboratory with outdated Russian instruments and agricultural textbooks that promised manna from heaven in just a few short weeks. We were preparing our bags when the doctor came into my room.

Antonio looked worried like he did the day we left the marina. Ever since then, he never looked quite the same, always pale and sweaty. But my mother said it was my imagination and wouldn't indulge me any further. Antonio asked if we wanted medical exemptions in order to take the month off, go fly-fishing in Cayo Largo if we wanted.

"Fly-fishing?" I was astonished. "We're not allowed to fish. We'll go to jail."

"Don't worry about what you can and cannot do, Uli. Do you want to skip camp this year or not?" my stepfather asked impatiently.

"Maybe we *should* take the month off," Nestor urged.

"You boys decide and let me know. Tarará isn't the safest place for you boys," he said. "It'll only take a couple of phone calls and you won't have to go digging in the dirt like some...like some...well, you decide."

"I don't think so. But thanks anyway," I rebuked the temptation.

Nestor continued stuffing bars of homemade lye soap and bottles of goat's milk shampoo in our bags, tacitly letting me know how upset he was that we couldn't go fly-fishing in Cayo Largo. He wrapped the strong smelling soap in the wrappers of the guest soaps he took from the marina. This would make them more salable. We kept the real Marina Hemingway soaps for ourselves, leaving them out of the wrapper so they'd desiccate; this was a post-revolution Cuban custom that would make the soap last longer.

I never really understood why voluntary workcamps were necessary, but Nestor's godfather, Guillermo, who was now living in Buenos Aires and was now known as William, explained to us one day why it was so important for us to volunteer, why it was our duty to attend whichever camp they sent us to each summer or winter break.

"Ulises, Nestor, come over here. Stop all this complaining! At your age, bah. That's just antisocial behavior!" After chastising us for not wanting to work in the fields, whether planting yucca or reaping soybeans, Guillermo explained that based on socialist ideals from around the world, *el trabajo voluntario* became the perfect resource for a Cuba that wished to develop as quickly as it could.

Cuba needed all of its people – young and strong people – to till soil, clear brush, and plant sugarcane. Proudly, thousands of future doctors, engineers, professors, and, of course, future politicians participated in some type of *trabajo voluntario* until around university age. So what were we complaining about?

Neither Nestor nor I cared about such things, we just knew there was rarely a break from school to play baseball or just hang out on our city block and whistle at the pretty girls who walked by without their older brothers.

It seemed that all we did, year after year, was take part in an educational project, a political or economic study, or simply attend a workcamp like this one in Tarará, all on a *voluntary* basis.

Guillermo did admit that it could be perceived that Cubans didn't know what we were doing, one summer planting sugarcane in the same field where we previously planted grass for cows to graze. Then, for some odd reason, we would replant sugarcane after clearing the fields of any grasses and weeds, only then realizing we needed to burn the sugarcane field before we started with tobacco on a new venture that would surely work.

No matter the circular mentality we rarely escaped, we worked so that equality and social justice prevailed, and we all knew that this would somehow magically improve our economy. After all, our economists and politicians believed, just as we did in each neighborhood of each province, that we could only fail but so many times before we got in the groove of being an independent State, independent of the support of the Soviet Union, that clearly ended after the fall, independent of the ideals that those exiled around the world held, independent of foreign currency that ebbed and flowed depending on the tourism markets around the world.

Yet we did this year after year, in rains or in drought. Because one day, we'd get it right!

"We could've gone back to the marina, *comemierda!*" my cousin scolded as he rat-tailed me with his towel. "Or gone to Cayo Largo or Jardines del Rey. Anywhere we wanted!"

"Did you forget what happened last time?"

Nestor paused as if trying to remember a dream he had just had minutes ago, but was now just a fleeting thought. "Maybe it was lightning hitting one of the piers," my cousin tried to reconcile. The memory of this event had already decayed. No mention of Zyrena, my dead siren.

"Nestor," I insisted, "we gotta go to the work camp. You know it's not right for the rest of our *compañeros* to go and for us just to hang around not doing our part." I felt that if I went back to our routines, went back to doing what was demanded of us in this special time, these last few weeks would magically reverse gears, and I would eventually forget everything we had seen at the marina complex.

"You're so full of shit, Uli," is all my cousin said as he continued packing, not understanding why I didn't want to accept Antonio's generous offer to skip camp this year.

Nestor was a survivor. I was a thinker. Slowly, I began not only to understand his bestial manner of thinking, but even worse, I began internalizing it.

Cubans like me can sometimes become so intoxicated with patriotism, as happens to so many people who don't have much else to become inebriated with, that we see what we are permitted to see and learn to become thankful for the few scraps of dignity pitched our way from the table of doctrine. This was a difficult charade to continue living, but it was my duty to shrug off these thoughts and my duty to protect Nestor.

For Nestor, ignorance was truly bliss. The marionette show that was his and our comrades' existences continued the phantasmagoria on the sidewalks of our province with no concern of anything occurring elsewhere, no concern of dreams or visions or frights or expectations. There were no philosophies tugging at his conscience, no history to convince him that this was the *only* way.

I thought of our new friends at Marina Hemingway. I wondered what Jean-Marc was doing. Was Uwe telling someone about his new friends, Uli and Nestor? Were José-María and Felipe sitting down this very moment to a steaming plate of *bacalao*? I couldn't remember what they looked like, even though it had just been a few weeks since we met these *turistas.* Did they survive the explosion?

What occurred that day at the marina did not affect the rest of the island at all. Well, I concluded that if we truly knew what occurred daily to keep this planet spinning, the shock would surely kill us. Our leader knew this and protected us from this heart-gripping terror. Most of us thanked him for this; others, as I soon learned in the U.S., despised him for this. Yet many would rather stare death and fear in the face than go around not knowing. Man's curiosity for other dimensions of reality can sometimes be deadly, but I soon realized it was our nature.

It's just like the old mares at *Parque Lenin*, a park dedicated years ago to rescuing old mares that were retired from breeding or racing. We used to visit these old horses when we were kids, often riding them for a few minutes around a small barn that kept these mares safe at night, safe from the many who would rather eat an old mare than be satisfied with the fact that, mostly for publicity, the mares would live their final days in peace.

Well, we learned when we were kids, when these mares' timeworn blinders are eroded and chewed away by the sun, the ethereal scope of vision of their new surroundings drives them crazy and makes them unmanageable. They crave their blinders and only until the stable keeper puts them back on do these mares calm down. Oftentimes, these mares are too old and too tired for such a shock, and it kills them on the spot.

I went to sleep thinking of the mares, thinking of how I used to visit them, wondering if any still existed. The tornadoes of thought swirling in my head continued battling each other, claiming victory only for an instant before another thought usurped its position. Curiosity, freedom, survival. What did this all mean? Was I even supposed to care at my age?

Thunder rolled through the night sky as my father's ghost appeared at the foot of my bed. Ulises was unchanged by the winds of time, uncaring of the millions of questions I always had. But that's all I remember before he dissolved into billions of stars, before he became just another speck in the whirlwind of my dreams.

I dreamed that I was at the marina again. My father was there. My mother, Graciela, was there kissing Antonio. She walked by Ulises and ignored him, but he didn't seem to care.

67

You know how dreams are. Those things that during the day seem implausible to us are perfectly sane when our eyes are closed.

Everyone was dancing, singing. I truly didn't care that the rest of my *compañeros* couldn't enter these pearly gates at the end of Jaimanitas to take part in the festivities. Our neighbors and schoolmates were beating down the gates of the Marina Hemingway complex, begging to come in. But I ignored them. What a relief not to care. Too bad this feeling couldn't last. Too bad guilt-laden philosophies would seep in with the morning's rays. Might as well enjoy it, I figured. One can't be blamed for what is experienced in dreams.

Then, as always, Nestor and I found Zyrena. Nestor wanted to do it with her right there. But, I talked him out of it and sent him home telling him he couldn't do a dead girl; he'd get diseases like polio or meningitis or something.

Then, after my cousin left the room, I noticed I didn't have any clothes on except for a pair of American-made Puma's. I had sold my clothes for this one pair of used sneakers, but nobody noticed. So, I pretended not to notice either.

All of a sudden, Zyrena got up and everybody started laughing at me for being fooled that she was dead. Music blared, and she began to sing her *bolero*. Even though she had a bullet hole in her head, she got up and told me how she was faking her death. She planned to escape the island in a coffin.

To make it up to me, she said she would give me a free kiss. She wanted me! I told Zyrena that I was sorry for letting her die. But she said not to worry about it since she really wasn't dead. She didn't seem to understand what I was saying.

I remembered I was naked, and I tried to cover myself, but it was to no avail. My heart beat out of my chest!

"*Ven aquí, Papito.*"

"What about Nestor? Don't tell him that you…"

"Does it matter?" she interrupted, placing a cold finger on my lips.

Her silky lips barely kissed my neck, my flushed cheeks. I asked her if I could kiss her. She said she couldn't wait.

68

"*Gracias*," is all I could whisper, feeling a bit ashamed that I had derived pleasure from her cold touch.

Then Mr. Mendelsen grabbed her from behind, ignoring me, as if I were a ghost or something.

The rest happened in slow motion. She fell to the floor dead, and I stood there naked and confused. The mares ran around me in circles.

CHAPTER 8

No one was up yet. I lay there thinking about my dream. About Zyrena. Was her face going to haunt me forever? Was my father's silence at the foot of my bed supposed to mean something?

I quickly got dressed and ran to Fortuna's house down the block for some answers. If anyone had answers about what my father had to tell me and what I had witnessed, Fortuna did.

I reached her house in less than a minute and rapped on the door.

"Fortuna, it's Uli." No one seemed to be awake. "Fortuna," I rapped on the door more persistently, *"Soy yo, Ulises."*

I was hoping she hadn't had a late night. Whenever she was up late, smoking her cigars and getting drunk with her gentlemen callers, she woke up in a shitty mood.

A lady answered the door in her tattered robe. It was Fortuna. Thank *la virgencita* she heard me. Fortuna wiped her eyes, her wiry hair standing at ends as if she had seen a spirit herself. Her light brown skin was spotted with hues of yellow and gray. She looked like a painter's pallet with paints everywhere waiting to be mixed. Yellow spots above her cheeks, a bit of reddish brown discoloration by her chin and even a bit of lavender-gray above her eyes.

"¿Niño, qué pasa?" she asked with solicitude. "Is everything all right?" she asked in her unique cat-like voice. She yawned, letting go of her guard and allowing her robe to briefly unveil her aging cleavage. Even half asleep, Fortuna could mesmerize you with her raspy, feline voice.

70

"I need to know some things," I begged standing outside her door.

"Come later, Uli. I can tell you anything you want later. Too tired right now. I doubt even the *Orísha* are awake at this ungodly hour. Besides, *un amiguito* slept over last night and..."

"Fortuna, *por favor*. I really need to know some things that only you seem to tap into. I wouldn't be bothering you or the *santos* this early if it weren't important."

Fortuna obliged, leaving the door open for me to come in. "You're as irresistible as your father was. No one could ever say no to Aguilera men. Just keep your voice down. I don't want to wake up Aníbal so early. We were both up very late."

She always kept a special place in her heart for my family and me. My father and his men used to come to her before being shipped out or before taking on a dangerous mission just for her blessings and spiritual cleansings. Or simply when they were lonely. Fortuna made things better, acted as an intercessor between them and *los santos*. She was the *madrina* of most of my father's friends, guiding them through hard times, advising them as to how to please their personal *Orísha,* or their personal saint, especially when frustration and disillusionment engulfed them. Fortuna always told them to embrace these feelings, especially any disillusionment they felt. Disillusionment, Fortuna always preached, was sacred.

Fortuna was a good teacher, a good *madrina*. She taught many people, including my father's men, that the *Orísha* go by many different names. They have their original, ancient names like *Changó, Yemayá, or Babalú Ayé*, and their Catholic saint counterparts. The *Orísha* also knew no gender gaps. For example, *Changó* is a male deity whereas his counterpart, Santa Barbara, is a female saint. It gets confusing, especially since most of us refer to the same deity or saint by different names in the same conversation, whether that be the Yoruba name or the Christian name. Whether it's a he in one world or a she in another world, this gender identity crisis didn't seem to preoccupy anyone in my country.

Fortuna taught them that each saint had to be greeted differently and ritualistically if one expected any favors from

71

him or her. Some were bowed to. Others, you had to lie on the floor before looking up at them. Then others, for some reason, just got a kiss on their plaster foreheads. Furthermore, each of these *Orísha* had different paths you must take. It was quite difficult to understand at times, but my comrades seemed not to have any problems reconciling these syncretic enigmas.

Bottles of homemade rum were everywhere. Obviously a party took place here last night. The room smelled like stale cigar smoke. I walked over to the kitchen window and opened it to let in some of the fresh air. Was it St. Lazarus' Day or the day of another important saint? No, she would have told me if it were one of the important Saint's Day, and I would've definitely heard if there were any *Changó* or *Babalú Ayé* parties going on around town.

"Do you want some coffee? I can't do a thing without my *cafecito*."

"*Sí, gracias, Fortuna.*" I responded sitting down at the dinette with the four multi-colored Haitian chairs. "No one makes *espumita* like you," I complimented.

"I'll only be a minute," she said as she tiptoed her way back into the bedroom as quietly as a kitten, probably to check on Aníbal.

I once asked her why she didn't have a matching set of chairs. She laughed as only she could, in that supercilious, purring way of hers. Nestor and I offered many times to come by and just paint them all one color. An eggshell white would've been nice.

"Don't you know that this is naïve art, Uli?"

"What's naïve about it?" I asked. She just laughed.

The four chairs represented the four solstices, she told me. Each had its own message and energy. Even though I wished I could take a paintbrush to them, to give her house a less eclectic look, I knew that she'd kill me if I touched her precious chairs.

Her former Haitian boyfriend, whom she always referred to as Didi, the one from Jiguaní, made these chairs especially for her many decades ago. He disappeared right before the

Revolution. Perhaps he went back to Haiti to craft more of these chairs.

I was sitting in the white polka-dotted chair with red and green serpents that swallowed their own tails. From a distance, they looked like Christmas balls painted on a background of white snow. I didn't appreciate this design much. It looked like a little kid painted it. The snakes were flat, no dimension to them at all, no expression. But these chairs were Fortuna's and she loved them so much.

There was a red chair with dragons that spit music notes instead of fire. This was obviously Fortuna's favorite as she always sat in this one whenever I visited.

The other chairs were green and yellow, respectively. The green one had scenes of people with baskets on their heads reaping a harvest. That one was my favorite. Even though the people had flat faces like the flat snake heads of the other chair, and their feet were not proportional with their bony bodies, this chair at least showed a scene of something I could grasp. Plus, the mountains and horizon looked very much like that of the Sierras. The legs of the harvest chair showed tiny pictures of women rolling and smoking cigars. The seat showed a woman breastfeeding while rolling a cigar on a straw mat.

The yellow chair showed a funeral procession with everyone dressed in white. Even though I felt that the artist should have had these people dressed in black, after all they were part of a funeral procession, Fortuna told me it was too hot in Haiti for anyone to wear black. The procession was a continuous chain from the back of the chair down to the legs.

I hated that chair! The corpse danced around with the mourners while they took him to be buried. That was just too weird and reminded me of the dream I had of Zyrena who wouldn't die. Besides why was the corpse so happy about being dead?

When Fortuna returned from the bedroom, she blessed the statue of Santa Barbara. I noticed the *santos* were not lit with their customary candles. Fortuna would certainly do that after making the coffee. Furthermore, voracious ants were attacking the pieces of cake and candy next to *el Santo Niño De Atocha*. In

73

Cuba, nothing goes to waste. If the boy Catholic saint counterpart of *Eleguá* with the red and black candle next to it didn't want the sweets, there were many voracious Cuban ants waiting for the libations.

"Tell me, Uli. Why on Earth are you coming to see me at this hour?" she asked with concern, placing the black and white *tacitas de café* on the table. "Is it another one of the visions of your father?" she mumbled in her raspy, nymph-like voice, yawning again but holding her robe tightly closed with her right hand lest I catch a glimpse. Her ebony eyes lowered as if listening to another voice in the room.

"Fortuna, it's not only the visions. Even though they've gotten strange," I confessed, the *espumita* as sweet and frothy as always. "My father now appears to me and just looks at me worriedly. Also…"

Fortuna interrupted me, "Shh, Uli. Shh. Your thoughts are muddling mine. Let me get the cowry shells. I'll be right back."

Good, she was getting the *caracoles*. They never held anything back. I waited in the dimly lit room witnessing Fortuna awaken the *Orísha* with candles. Ringing a bell, as if waking the gods for school, she borrowed the *caracoles* from a copper bowl set next to gray, polished stones.

Fortuna put a red scarf over her nappy hair and sat in front of me in the red chair with the music-breathing dragons.

"Before I even look at what the cowry shells tell me, I tell you this. Be careful. Be very careful. The *Orísha* tell me you don't know what you've stumbled upon. Not even your father can protect you from what you've discovered." Fortuna looked serious.

"*Vamos a ver, Papito,*" she whispered shaking the cowries in her hand before throwing them on the table like an experienced gambler shooting craps. "You've seen too much, too soon. *Los santos* aren't sure why you've been shown all that you've been shown. This can't be right."

She picked up the *caracoles* again and threw them on the table, this time with a slight flick of the wrist. "Sometimes even *los caracoles* need two out of three," she laughed.

74

"What do they say, Fortuna? C'mon, tell me what the cowry shells say."

"There is discord amongst them. I've never seen the *Orísha* so confused. They're trying to figure out which one of them led you down this path. *Changó* is being blamed. He defends his stance to let you see what you will. He's very much like you – sees the world in black and white, right and wrong. He says it's the only way to make things right. I see him holding you and putting a rubber band around you."

"A rubber band, Fortuna?" I asked incredulously. "Why would Santa Barbara do that?"

"Shh! Clearly there's a higher purpose here. 'This is the only way,' he pleads with the rest of the *Orísha*."

"The only way for what?"

"That's all he says. But wait! *Oshún* and *Babalú Ayé* are at each other's throats, fighting to protect you as well. They each believe that the future shouldn't be meddled with. They believe *Changó* shouldn't have meddled. I've never seen this kind of battle in my life. I never knew it was possible for them to fight among each other this way."

"Did I do something to piss them off, Fortuna?"

"I really don't know, Uli. I don't even know if this has anything to do with you. I think you're just caught up...wait," she said as she threw the cowries on the table once more, softly this time almost as if trying to balance a fragile piece of glass. She covered the cowries and rolled them with the palm of her hand. She spoke Yoruba, clicking her tongue a few times.

Almost singing the words, *"Odun tiatibi mi sinu ki e bami ye ojo iku fun ara mi ati awon omo mi ti mo bi. Kiamaku ni kekere, kiamaku iku ina, kiamaku iku oro, kiamaku ike ejo, kiamaku sinu omi."*

I didn't understand a word she was saying. She continued, "Avert death for all my children, avert death for all those I include in my prayers. May they not die young, may they not die in fire, may they not die in tragedy, may they not die in shame, may they not die in water."

"Die?" I asked. "Who's going to die?'

75

Fortuna ignored me and continued her prophecy, "He's always been there for you. They've all agreed to protect you as much as they can regardless of *Changó's* actions to change the future."

"Protect me from what?" I whispered.

"Uli, is this true? What did you do my boy? Please tell me you didn't. This is quite serious. What did you see, *Papito*? It has death all over it," she said charismatically shaking her shoulders and snapping her fingers over her head, then over mine.

"The doctor..."

"No, no. Not the doctor. In fact, he's helping you. You saw something else. This person needs prayer to find her way to peace. I'll light a candle for her. Who was she?"

"Fortuna, you should know that..."

"No, never mind. I don't want to know. I don't like what I know already. *¡Solavaya!*"

She picked up the shells again and shook them with her eyes closed. In that irresistible cat-like voice of hers, she continued speaking Yoruba. I sat there waiting for some answers, watching the sunrise through her kitchen window.

"You need protection," she advised giving me a red and black beaded necklace. "Keep this on *siempre*." Fortuna continued speaking in this familiar African dialect. It looked as if she was blessing the *eleke* beads. Then, she kissed it and placed it around my neck.

"Don't let anyone touch it. Don't let anyone take it off you."

"Fortuna, just let me tell you what happened."

Ignoring me, Fortuna warned: "Remember, the *Orisha* are confused. That's very strange. But, they're all on your side now because of their miscalculation. They have no choice but to protect you from their mistake. It's just that they've meddled with the future and now the past and present are rolling all over you like an earthquake trying to catch up with what's been reset as your fate. Just listen to them."

"How? How am I supposed to understand?"

76

"Do you hear what the *caracoles* are saying? Your journey has just begun. It will take you far. Very far. You have no control over this journey, so don't fight it. However, you'll be safe as long as you act on instinct, act quickly. May God forgive me, but sometimes the *santos* act as foolishly and recklessly as children. As primordial as they are, they sometimes are imprudent."

"Act how? What's going on? I'm more confused now than when I came here this morning. If *Changó* screwed up, why am I paying for it?"

"It's not for us to question. Just move through the journey with the gods' help. Move on without asking why or arguing with them. We sometimes argue effectively, too effectively, and it confuses the *Orísha*, especially *Changó* who is weak to practical arguments."

"You're speaking in riddles. What journey? Am I going back to the marina?" I needed to know.

"You'll know. You'll know what to do. But more importantly," she grabbed my hand, "you'll know when to do nothing." Fortuna looked at me with her radiant black eyes and smiled. "Sometimes it is important just to be still and think or do nothing."

"OK, Fortuna, I'll do my best," I said, still confused about all she was telling me.

"You look just like your father when he used to come see me. Always wanting to know the answers to life's most enigmatic mysteries. Always wanting to know the outcome even before *los santos* knew the outcome themselves. It'll be all right, Uli. It'll be all right." She held my hand. "What are you doing today?"

"Nestor and I are going to work in Tarará."

"Come by after you're through. How long? A couple of weeks?"

"Almost a month."

"I need to give you a good *despojo*; you need a good spiritual cleansing. Bring me all the white flowers you can find. I have some witch hazel and some *agua florida*. Bring me some

77

river water, water from a green coconut, and I'll get the rest for the sacred bath."

"Do I need to drink chicken's blood or sacrifice a goat?" I asked, not wanting to offend the *Orísha* by leaving without some sort of offering.

"If you can still find a goat in Cuba, by all means eat it, baby. Sacrifice a goat," she bent over with her feline laughter, "in Cuba! *¡Ay mi niño!*" Tears came to her eyes as she laughed at my question. Her cheekbones shined with glee as I apparently started her morning off with a good joke.

"The *Orísha* understand Cubans can no longer afford these sacrifices. We're not in Miami where they could afford sacrificing the best meat, no wads of fat and bone to trick the gods. The *Orísha* have settled for prayer and fasting. I've gotta tell Cuca that you wanted to sacrifice a goat! You're adorable, Uli. All you gotta do is come visit me more often. Not only when you have a problem. You'll be fine, *mi vida*, everything will work out for you no matter how scary life becomes."

"*Gracias*, Fortuna."

"Before I forget, take this."

"What is it?" I asked taking a small velvet pouch that was sewn shut.

"It's for protection," she nodded, urging me that it was all right. "Just don't ever open it, Uli. God knows what will happen if you open it."

"Thank you, Fortuna. You don't know how much I appreciate you."

"*Ay niño*, go. You don't want to be late."

We both heard rumbling coming from her bedroom warning us Aníbal, her newfound friend, was awake.

"Go!" she pushed me out the door and tightened her scarf. She obviously wanted time to fix herself up before Aníbal saw her in the morning light.

I left Fortuna's house still not certain if everything would turn out fine. I should've told her what I knew. But the less she knew the better. No sense in putting Fortuna in any danger. She waved goodbye to me through her kitchen window, singing a song about an artist who only painted pink angels and forgot to paint black cherubs. Fortuna was strange, but I'm glad I knew her.

I felt the necklace around my neck and the velvet pouch in my hand. As much as I wanted to believe that this is all I needed, aside from the spiritual bath, my spirit was restless.

The velvet pouch felt like it had a cross, a chicken's foot, and small stones inside. I knew I couldn't open it to find out what was in it. I'd die or something. Well, maybe Nestor and I would muster the courage to take a quick peek and then sew it back up without the *Orísha* noticing.

CHAPTER 9

"Uli, don't forget the soap," Nestor said looking out the window and seeing the *camello* with many of our troupe members already on it. On the lid of a cardboard box, written in permanent black marker, the bus had "Troupe 476 – Tarará" posted on the front right hand side of its windshield. This was the one for us! If we were late, someone would have to drive us, or worse, we'd have to hitch a ride.

The morning bus ride to Tarará took almost an hour as the streets were still rivers of mud and rock. Nestor got bored and endeavored to sell the extra bars of soap he packed to our comrades who naïvely expected these basic necessities would be provided to them by the camp guards.

"Where were you this morning?" my cousin asked as he passed a bar of soap to Nicolas, Pedro's youngest brother.

"With Fortuna."

"For a *despojo*?" my cousin goofed, waving his hands in the air as if spirits were possessing him. "I see a bright future ahead," taunted Nestor, putting his hands on his forehead as if falling into a trance; the entire busload of boys roared with laughter. He turned his eyelids inside out and starting walking like Frankenstein down the narrow bus aisle.

"Keep making fun of *los santos*, Nestor."

"What's this?" he pulled at my necklace.

"Don't touch it. You know you're not supposed to touch it, *sapingo!*"

As I pulled away from Nestor's grasp, he didn't let go in time and the red and black beads flew into the air, bouncing all over the floor of the bus. Everyone gasped.

80

"You really believe in that stuff?" Nestor questioned, his eyebrows always pointing up when he felt superior.

"*Lo tengo trabaja'o,*" I warned. "You know what can happen now?" I fretted, trying to see how many of the beads I could salvage. But this was to no avail. The beads fell through every crevice of the old bus.

Nestor quickly took his hands and superstitiously wiped them on Pedro's back. This quickly unfolded into a game of who had the spiritual cooties that didn't end until somebody stuck his elbow in Nestor's eye.

"*¡Coño!*" Nestor shouted at Albertico who quickly crouched next to the flat emergency tire in the back of the bus, afraid of the repercussions that would ensue for elbowing Nestor.

Everyone grew quiet waiting for Nestor's next step. Realizing all eyes were on him, he broke into laughter. Everyone, even the bus driver, took a deep sigh of relief that he didn't have to stop the bus in a hurry on these muddy roads; the tension was broken.

Nestor had obviously taken command of this bus, this troupe. It was bound to happen that someone took commanding rank. After all, we couldn't have anarchy. By the time we reached Tarará, all the boys tacitly understood their roles for the next month. There was always an order of socialization at these camps that went unspoken and was established early, many times even before we arrived.

The weak ones, like Albertico, were always spotted immediately; they were usually the tenderfoots or the ones who never fought back. These comrades would be the ones to be picked on and pushed around for the rest of the month, sometimes even made to be the camp housekeepers taking care of duties that our mothers usually handled. Nothing difficult, just picking up around the barracks so as not to receive troupe demerits for untidiness, or if the person was truly weak, they were made to wash our shorts from the inevitable emissions that occurred throughout the evening.

These ranks were accompanied with nicknames. This wasn't unique to the work camp by any means. Cubans had a way of nicknaming those around us, regardless of age, not out of

81

spite or anger, but more out of a sign of familiarity or kinship. Unless you're Cuban or have known many Cubans, there is no relating the significance of this re-christening process.

There was *El Morito*, the Lebanese-Cuban; *Roberto Clemente*, the kid who would represent the under-fifteen group in the Pan-American Games. Albertico became *El Codo*, since he struck Nestor in the eye with his elbow. Then there was *El Enamora'o* who pined for his girlfriend throughout the entire bus trip. *El Bizco, Fumeco*, and *El Poeta* were also among the group as well as *Jirafa* with his long neck.

Even Nestor and I did not escape this christening. Nestor, who arrived with a black eye and a big bump because of *El Codo's* clumsiness, was known as *El Cíclope*. I immediately took on *El Santo* even though I was by no means an initiated follower of Santeria, but the now-broken red and black beaded necklace was enough to pigeonhole me as such.

Even though we didn't know one another because of the gerrymandering of my district, we knew each other now!

Tarará looked different from the last time Nestor and I were there. A *fábrica* had been built in the valley below our barracks and adjacent to the fields where we would work. The camp leaders made it quite clear that this newly erected factory was off limits to anyone. When we asked what it was for, we always received different answers. Some said it was for the processing of the yucca and malanga that would hopefully grow here by next year if the rains ever let up. Other camp leaders said it was an oil refinery. Then there were those who simply told us it was not for us to question.

The rain was incessant. However, we didn't mind as this meant settling in our bunks without anything to do. It would be like a small vacation in the countryside, a vacation that allowed us to continue taunting and badgering our peers.

Everyone immediately claimed his bunk. Even though our names were on the bunks already, if someone wanted your bunk and you couldn't fight for it, your name came off. Most of us wanted the top bunks. I don't know why. I guess it felt as if there was more privacy up there. Not everyone could manage to get these, so some of us had to settle for the bottom bunks.

There were thirty other bunks in a barracks that should hold no more than fifteen. They were pushed together to form one giant top bunk, thirty beds wide, and one giant lower bunk of the same length. As much as we attempted to move the bunks at least a couple of centimeters apart, it was to no avail as the barracks were only so wide.

They told us that in the morning we would be served breakfast, which usually consisted of *pan de boniato* and a cup of watered-down soy or rice milk. This was a warning not to be late, and it was the most efficient way they knew of to get us up on time. Anyone who had been to the camps before knew that if you didn't eat the Cuban sweet potato bread as soon as it came out of the oven, you could only use it as a doorstop.

It was truly miraculous. When it was hot, it was soft and sweet. However, as soon as the Cuban humidity hit it, it metamorphosed into the hardest material known to man. Nestor said that they sometimes used this bread in wars when soldiers ran out of artillery. No one believed him of course. However, we all agreed that some of the *campesinos* used these loaves as bricks out in the country.

With the sun setting, some of the kids started playing canasta. *El Poeta* began writing his poems to the many *señoritas* awaiting him back in El Vedado. *Fumeco* joined Nestor by setting up a small table next to the black and white TV to continue selling the soap my cousin had smuggled in; *Fumeco* sold his American cigarettes. It proved to be a profitable endeavor for both of them, even though the cigarettes were incredibly weak in comparison to Cuban *cigarrillos*.

Most of us didn't have any American dollars, but *Fumeco* and Nestor still made out like bandits by bartering for camp services. *El Enamora'o* promised to tend to *Fumeco's* bunk for the rest of the month in exchange for three cigarettes a day. *El Morito* took on the same chore for Nestor, if Nestor made sure to save enough soap for him to take back to his mother whose birthday was coming up. I just hung out watching the canasta players, whispering to *El Bizco* how he should play his hand.

"This isn't poker," *El Bizco* told me, his eyes crossing every time he got nervous or got riled up.

"Yeah," interrupted *Jirafa*. "Either join in or shut up."

"Fuck you!" I said, an expression I had learned from an American uncle who had visited us a long time ago. An expression that sounded so vulgar yet proper at times.

"*Fokee ju*, too!" *Jirafa* tried to repeat. Everyone laughed.

I went to the window and noticed three of the guards on their way to our barracks. This was strange that they would leave the comfort of the officers' barracks to traverse the rain. No matter how important it was, it could certainly wait until morning. Unless our bunks were bugged and they knew about the little capitalism my cousin and *El Fumeco* were developing.

"*Oye! Oye!* They're coming. Put all that stuff away. Three of them are coming!" I warned my comrades.

"Put that away," my cousin told *El Fumeco*. "Now!"

People scurried like organized ants, hiding soap, cigarettes, dirty Vietnamese magazines, and extra sets of underwear under the worn, dingy mattresses. Most of us nervously gathered around the canasta table.

"*¡Atención!*" one of the leaders barked after busting through the door.

"*¡Atención!*" repeated my cousin to show that he was on their side and the elected leader of the troupe.

"We don't need your help, *gracias*."

"Sorry," Nestor said. "Just trying to maintain some..." he knew he better shut up by their sneers.

"We have a very important announcement. During your stay, things are going to change a little bit. We have just received news that *El Líder* himself will visit Tarará with his brother, Raúl."

Everyone gasped. Castro himself was going to visit us here. There were mixed feelings in all of us. Did this mean extra work for us to show him that our generation was as committed to his demands and progress as was the generation who placed him in power? Did this mean that TV cameras were going to come along with him? If so, we were lucky because we'd be sure to receive gloves for digging, fresh food, and showers every day.

Our leader continued, "It is necessary that you show him and his brother how hard you work. But more importantly, it is necessary that you show him that you are good *pioneros* who know not to ask questions and who know not to complain."

"Like about the factory in the valley below?" blurted *El Poeta*. Poets were always stupid like that, keeping quiet when they shouldn't and speaking their thoughts when it was not called for.

"Who are you?" demanded to know one of the camp guards.

"That's *El Poeta*," answered his colleague. Everyone laughed that the officer knew our comrade's nickname.

"*El Poeta*. Our own José Martí! Well, *El Comandante* will be proud. Listen, *Poeta*, I suggest you stick with your poetry and not worry about the factory." Turning to all of us after placing his hands on *El Poeta's* shoulders, "This is exactly what I mean. When he visits, there will be no questions like this. The factory is his concern, and we have nothing to do with it. Furthermore, there will be a luncheon provided by him and Raúl where the President will speak to you for approximately twenty minutes."

Luncheon and speech, there would be cameras for sure.

"Will he help us till the soil?" *El Poeta* said again, ignoring the soldier's hand heavily placed on his shoulder. "After all, true socialists have no differences in class, duties, and respect." No one laughed this time. *El Poeta* had gone too far.

Without a word, two of the men grabbed our *compañero*, dragging him out into the stormy night. Damn fool couldn't keep his trap shut. Why didn't he save it for his journal? No one said a word as it was obvious that he was going to be made the example for any of us who thought we could speak out and question the State.

El Poeta screamed and kicked, but the men showed no hesitation or remorse. To them, he was just a sniveling kid who needed discipline. Being the first day, someone was bound to be made the example.

After the loud-mouthed poet was dragged out of the barracks, "Before I continue, is there anyone else that would like

85

to join their comrade?" The group remained silent, except for the Russian cartoons emitting from the black-and-white TV near my bunk. "I didn't think so. There will be guests with him. Important guests from Hungary and Russia, maybe even China, but that's still unclear," the soldier looked at his notes.

Looking back up, "They're thinking of turning this camp into a vineyard using Hungarian soil. *El Presidente* has invested a lot of money for our future. The Hungarian soil will produce fine Cuban wines for exportation. This will bring in necessary funds for our country. Needless to say, these foreign diplomats will be very impressed by meeting you as their first workers on the vineyard. Don't disappoint us or them."

I raised my hand ever so gently, not to provoke any argument, "Are we no longer going to till the soil for yucca?"

"No, this plot of land will only be tilled for grapes. We will explain more as soon as the weather lets up. But first the soil has to be prepared with the appropriate nitrates to enrich the Hungarian soil. The new Agricultural Minister will also come down to run some tests."

They told us what they thought we should know and left us alone for the rest of the evening.

A few seconds after they left our cabin, we heard *El Poeta's* screams. He sounded like a cat shrieking in the night. There were laughs of drunken men, more screams and crying, and then silence. We tried to get to the window to see what was happening, but they had taken him below our view. What were they doing to him? Were they beating him senseless? Poets weren't very popular in my country, unless, of course, they worked for the State.

Nestor looked at me and nodded as if saying, *These bastards shouldn't get away with this.* I agreed without saying a word.

"¡*Hijos de puta!*" someone shouted from the back of the room, breaking the silence that contained us in fright.

"Where do you think they'll take him?" whimpered Albertico.

"Who knows?" I said. "Who knows what they will do to him."

"It's for the good of the State," mumbled *Jirafa*.

"You're crazy, *acere*," *El Bizco* attacked, his eyes more cockeyed than ever. "He's our friend!"

Talks about what was right and wrong were tossed around the barracks all night. Nothing was resolved. Some of the troupe thought that insubordination was the beginnings of anarchy. And anarchy could not be tolerated at any level. Then there were those, of whom I was more and more becoming a part, who felt that if one has to force things to happen, silence those who do not agree, then perhaps we're fighting a losing battle, a battle people stopped fighting ages ago.

We all went to our bunks, smoking the cigarettes *El Fumeco* had sold us and listening to the rain. That was the last time anyone saw *El Poeta* again. I mean anyone.

I walked over to *El Poeta's* bunk and etched his name. It wasn't enough that his name, his spirit, would always be etched in my memory. Memories fade and get rewritten, and someone needed to create physical proof that our friend existed. I had always been somewhat intolerant of those who talked against the State. I felt that my father would've wanted it that way. But *El Poeta* was one of my newest friends.

Trying to forget what occurred, we made a list (my cousin's idea), giving us each time alone with the Vietnamese magazine. Nestor was first, as he came up with the idea of taking turns. I was dead last. Magazine and all, I still couldn't put my loud-mouthed friend out of my mind.

We were later told *El Poeta* was sent to another camp where Castro would not visit. But we soon found out that not even his mother, who was terrified to ask what happened, saw him again.

Chances are the guards themselves did not know. In cases like this, insurrectionists were just passed down from one group of guards to the other, each group coming up with another punishment for the backslidden Cuban. Before you knew it, no one remembered who tortured the boy last. Everyone would just point fingers and the State would have to sweep the whole thing up under the proverbial rug, afraid their perverse incompetence would be divulged.

87

Is this what my father fought for? A bunch of drunken officers being able to take out their frustrations on a fifteen-year-old poet? Did my father know that the State's tactics were to murder those, even kids, who dared speak out against the government? If so, what was the difference between this system and the former Batista regime? My head began swirling with these thoughts.

I knew, and often agreed, that those rising up violently against the demands of the Revolution should be dealt with harshly, without mercy. After all, violence and revolutions are inseparable. We were all taught early on that the security of the people – whether that be moral or political – was the important thing. No action would be tolerated that would undermine the security of the majority. But *El Poeta* was my friend, and it just didn't seem right.

He just had a big mouth; I bet he didn't even know what he was saying. But, after all, this was the only way to maintain the Revolution's ideals. Did *El Poeta* really prove to be a threat against the establishment? Could a fifteen-year-old represent such subservience that torture and death were the only solution? I was really confused and got a headache that pounded till I closed my eyes. I postponed my time with the Vietnamese rag, claiming double time the next day as I was sure I'd be up for it then.

I lay in my bed thinking that I was becoming one of *them*. One of the *gusanos* whom I had learned to hate so much. I didn't want to be a worm like those who had been fleeing my country for decades, but my disillusionment was becoming palpable. I wish I knew what Fortuna meant by disillusionment being sacred. It certainly didn't feel like that at all. My disillusionment just manifested itself with a corporeal lump in my throat that was close to choking me.

I loved my country. My country was beautiful, charismatic. It vibrated with the history of *criollos* fighting for independence. But it also showed the wisdom of its revolution on the broken backs of so many Cubans. I wondered if I learned what other crazy things went on in my country would drive me mad. The blindfold of childhood was coming off quickly, and I was truly afraid that the shock of my father dying in vain, the shock of being a young man in Cuba, would kill me.

I only had one dream all night long that played like a looping video. This was strange as I usually dreamed seven or eight times a night. But that night, I only dreamed of the old mares at *Parque Lenin* with their brownish-gray coats and timeworn blinders.

They trotted around a fire, not realizing that they stood in the same place for hours, thinking their master was taking them on a mile trot to keep their old muscles strong. The trotting, like hollow coconuts banging against the pavement, became louder and louder synthesizing with the downpour outside my bunk, deafening me in my sleep.

I felt my heart palpitate faster and faster. Then, Fortuna stood there with the horses speaking in Yoruba, clicking her tongue and spitting tobacco juice all over the San Lázaro icon that stood on crutches with ceramic dogs licking its glazed wounds. She blew cigar smoke at the horses that neighed at the smell of the aromatic Cuban tobacco.

I didn't understand what she was doing there, but she was with the living *Virgen de la Caridad del Cobre, Oshún* herself, nonchalantly talking as if no one could see that it was really Our Lady under all those robes. But I knew. Was I supposed to know? As the rain kept beating the old mares, their visors gradually slipped. I wanted to scream, but I remained frozen in sleep.

Why weren't Fortuna and *La Caridad* doing something to protect these mares? Instead of trying to safeguard these frail, wet horses against the reality of it all, they were more worried about keeping the fire going, as if the mares were not really there, not their concern.

They were letting them die!

"*Oye*, Fortuna, look! Help them keep their blinders on." They ignored me. They just looked at me as if they couldn't understand why I was getting so upset. They were making me feel stupid for being so anxious. Yet I couldn't help but scream at them, even at Our Lady herself, for not helping the old mares.

89

But there they stood, Fortuna and *La Caridad* chatting away, oblivious to the mares' panic.

One by one, the ragged visors hit the ground. The mares rammed into each other forgetting their choreographed rain dance around the fire. Blood spewed forth from some of their eyes. Some of them simply ran off the nearby precipice. I could hear them drowning in the murky Almendares River, their lungs filling with water as they neighed to Our Lady's deaf ears, their carcasses being washed away into the Straits of Florida.

Others simply rolled around the ground or pounded their old gray heads against the Spanish mahogany trying to inch their blinders back on, as if scratching an irresistible itch that just wouldn't be ameliorated. But it was to no avail. The rain melted their visors off their heads. No matter which way these animals ran or which way they collapsed to try and cover their heads with the surrounding mud, there was no fighting the panoramic images that bombarded them in the storm.

Fortuna and *Cachita* applauded as if they were watching some show, desensitized to the old mares' suffering. Then, the park was suddenly empty except for Fortuna, Our Lady, who was now dipping her feet in the Almendares, and me. There was no storm, no blood, no drowning mares.

Without saying a word to me, Fortuna and Our Lady assured me with their eyes that this was the way things were.

They patted me on the back as if I had done something brave by standing there and letting these mares die without their blinders, letting these mares die free of any illusions. It was a positive thing, precious or sacred even. But I still didn't understand what they meant.

The rain continued beating on the tin roof of the barracks as I replayed the dream again and again. Sure, each time was a little different, but the mares always died from the shock of it all. I did't understand how that could be precious or sacred.

I heard the TV on in the barracks as I tossed and turned. My comrades left it on for its luminescence, and the sounds coming from the cartoons, although we could barely understand Russian, comforted us. My father did not appear to me, nor did

Changó who Fortuna claimed was on my side. I didn't even think of *El Poeta*. I only thought of the old mares at Lenin Park out in the rain trying to maintain their ripped blinders from divulging more than they could bear.

CHAPTER 10

The next few days at the Tarará camp went as expected. We never knew when the President would show up, so they had us on our toes, ready for anything. We even practiced running to the showers and back to ensure that we'd be clean at a moment's notice.

The guards gave us new clothes with red kerchiefs to wear around our necks. They promised us we could keep these uniforms as a gift. These came with polished badges that gave our troupe an official identification number, troupe number 476, and the honor of *avanzado* right above the number and embroidered on our red kerchiefs, an honor only given to *pioneros* who had participated in many cultural activities, many parades, many picture opportunities.

These new uniforms were to be worn after our showers when *El Presidente* was nearby; no need for cameras from around the world to see his little *pioneros* in ripped up, soiled camp-wear. And we were proud of these. They looked sharp!

The rains continued on and off, making it easier to till the land. Usually, when it came to cultivating, the ground was as hard as Italian marble in Tarará. Not having the proper machines or beasts to aid in this task made our hands bleed. This was seen as an admirable trait to the leaders of the camp, giving certificates to those whose hands showed the most calluses at the end of the month. Guess there wouldn't be any certificates for rough hands and bleeding palms this summer, but we did have the *avanzados* medals that proved more valuable and honorable than any other kind.

92

All we had to do was rid the soil of rocks so the next group of youngsters could begin preparing the soil with the proper nitrates that would allow the Hungarian soil to adapt to our Caribbean climate; at least that's what they hoped for.

Albertico had had enough, crying all night for his parents, crying because his hands were sore, crying because he had the runs, crying when we picked on him for crying. Ugh, it was a never-ending cycle. So we told him if he wanted to convince the doctors to give him a leave from the camp, he had to do what so many of his comrades had done before, what so many future Olympic medalists, engineers, doctors, and astronauts had dared to do to get out of life in *el trabajo voluntario*. It wasn't the patriotic thing to do, but I just had it with his whining and crying.

There were certain tricks of the trade for those not willing to put up with the demands of the voluntary work camp. These were unwritten recipes, if you will, passed down in the oral tradition from fathers to sons.

One way to be sent home was to infect your eyes. This was quite easy. You could put dirt or dust in your eyes, making you wake up with a bad case of conjunctivitis. Fearing this would spread, albeit knowing it was self-inflicted, the camp medics let you go home as if you really had contracted pink eye.

However, the smart medics would make you wash your eyes out and wait a day or so in isolation. If the symptoms cleared up, which they usually did if you only used dirt or dust, then back to the camp you went with a small bottle of tobramycin. If there were no tobramycin or other antibiotics to be found, that usually being the case, the medics applied a honeybee venom extract with a cold washcloth. If this wasn't available either, the medics would boil salt in water, let it cool and then make you rinse your eye with the brine; they called this hydrotherapy and it burned like hell.

Nestor discovered from talking to kids who had successfully been released from camp that the best way to give yourself an acute bacterial eye infection was to take cobwebs on your index finger and clog your lachrymal ducts with the sticky silk. It itched and burned, I was told, but it worked! For some

93

reason, this gave people the worst infections, causing yellow pus to ooze from the eyes, which blew up like bloodshot ping-pong balls. The tobramycin they'd give you didn't work on this type of infection. But if you wanted out badly enough and were afraid to follow any of the other recipes, this was the way to go. Plus you could then sell the tobramycin *por la izquierda* and make some real cash.

Another way to be sent home, more severe but definitely not the most drastic, was to fracture your arm or foot. This sounds painful, but there were ways to get around the pain. Don't get me wrong, this must have hurt like hell too, probably more than the hydrotherapy, but it was a winner of an idea.

Nestor says this is why our friend from the block, Eliades, always claimed his arm hurt on rainy days like these. According to Nestor, Eliades successfully fractured his arm at the age of eight just to be able to go back home. Not sure that's worth all that much pain!

Eliades told Nestor it was easy. At night, before going to sleep, he took a T-shirt and soaked it in water. The trick was to keep the T-shirt wet all night. This wasn't too difficult as the humidity was always cooperative. Then, Eliades wrapped the T-shirt tight around his arm. You could use your foot too. In the morning, Eliades's arm was clammy and moist. He said he could feel the moisture deep in the marrow, softening the bones. Then a comrade, in his case *Radio Bemba*, a *compañero* we all know who loved to gossip about everything, took a brick or stone (if your aim was your foot, you lifted the bunk and placed your foot underneath) and – wham!

One shot is all it took and, Eliades claimed, you hardly felt a thing, until a few hours later when you wished you had toughed out the work camp instead of crushing your foot or arm. Still, there are kids who just won't stay at camp for whatever reason and do this.

Girls could always get away with saying they had a nervous condition or fake a hemorrhage with pig's blood from the kitchen. Most of the medics or nurses were men and wouldn't dare keep a girl who was bleeding from her vagina at camp. No way! So, they had it pretty easy.

94

If no blood was available, though, they had to rely on the nervous condition routine. All they had to do was cry and pretend they heard voices. They'd be sent home with tranquilizers and a referral to see the province's psychiatrist. Big deal. The town psychiatrist usually gave them Xanax or Rufinols which, in turn, the girls could sell in the black market for mega bucks, proving very profitable to them – even though the girls would be classified as schizophrenic or prone to psychotic episodes in the government files.

When pretending to hear voices, though, they had to make sure not to say they heard a dead relative's voice or the voices of the *Orísha*. This would not be taken as a simple case of schizophrenia. Oh no! This called for having someone like Fortuna come down to the camp and interpret the messages from beyond. This called for letting all the higher-ups know what was occurring so they could ask special favors from the saint or ancestor.

My mother, Graciela, had a friend they called *La Monjita* who pretended to hear messages from *la Virgen de Regla*. What a mistake this was, my mother told me. The girl was kept at camp even beyond the compulsory period because the guards wanted to hear what the saint's messages were. Even Fidel Castro came down to ask for the saint's blessings for a prosperous country. He was also having women troubles, Graciela said.

Poor girl couldn't be diagnosed as a schizophrenic no matter how possessed she acted. She was given her own barracks, though, with sweet potatoes, desserts made from coconut, fresh mangos, tamarind, mamey apples, apple bananas, and anything else *La Monjita* craved. They even gave her *Yemayá's* favorite, pork crackling, which was difficult to come by. Graciela said they all ate so well that summer!

Albertico wouldn't go through with any of these ideas. So, Nestor came up with a plan. It would be easy as pie. Someone should go to the clinic and fake a headache, stomachache, or something. When the nurse turned around or left the room, he would swipe a needle. One of the small ones, we assured Albertico. Once back, we'd inject Albertico in his foot or hand, someplace easy like that, with mud or kerosene from the lamps. The doctors wouldn't dare keep a boy at camp with a black ball growing out of his arm. On his way home, he could take the needle and suck the mud or kerosene back out. He'd be watching cartoons back home before he knew it, not just the Russian or Mexican ones we saw here at camp, but the North Korean ones, which were pretty cool just because these were so hard to figure out.

Albertico was hesitant at first, changing his mind and saying he would go for the pink eye, not with the cobwebs though. But Nestor, eager to try a new method and truly hoping it would work so future generations would sit around at camp saying a great man named Nestor came up with this, convinced Albertico that he knew someone who went blind from sticking dirt in his eye. Did he want to go blind?

Albertico gulped at the thought of spending the rest of his life with no sight. If he ever proved to be a useless *compañero,* they'd put him away and no one would ever hear from him again; after all, what good would he be to the community?

He reconsidered the broken foot or arm routine, but Nestor convinced him that the guards had seen that millions of times. And if it didn't work the first time, Nestor warned him, we'd have to keep pounding away until the bone cracked. It sometimes took twenty, thirty whacks with a brick or coconut to break the bone, my cousin said, which was a lie as the rest of us knew it always broke with the first whack if the limb was damp enough.

"OK," Albertico nodded with pursed lips as if knowing he was making the right decision, "who's going to go get the needle?"

Nestor immediately volunteered hoping he could scrounge up some real aspirin, cough syrup, and other goodies that would prove valuable in the black market. His parents would be upset, yet they would accept the money once it came in. A bottle of aspirin could get up to ten American dollars. This seemed like highway robbery but when you consider hospitals in

96

la yuma charge even more, Nestor was just fomenting competition.

I suggested that we didn't use kerosene or mud. This seemed primitive, at the very least unsanitary. Instead, we should use petroleum or tar. Once, my mother's friend's nephew, Juan-Carlos, injected tar between his anklebone and skin so he could get off the island. The doctors couldn't figure out what the black growth was and were afraid that some sort of Black Plague would spread over the island. The authorities expedited the man's papers and let his family in Miami bring him to the U.S.

I told the troupe about this, and they all agreed that if this man did it, so could Albertico. Nestor was upset that he hadn't heard of this story.

"It was basically my idea, you just built on it," my cousin kept repeating.

My cousin was properly credited with the idea, and I insisted Nestor and I would split up. When he went to the nurse, I would run down to the factory we were supposed to stay away from. They'd have some sort of tar or petrol chemical just sitting around. A small amount missing would go unnoticed.

The rains pounded Nestor and me as we went in opposite directions. *¡Pa' la patria!* We shouted to each other, as if we were going on a covert mission for the fatherland. The guards were not going to leave their barracks, not in this inclement weather and not since the leader brought them a few bottles of Havana Club rum as a gift from the factory visitors. We were on our own for the rest of the night.

CHAPTER 11

I rolled down the hill in case anyone was watching. I could always say I was dared to roll down the hill or something childish like that and probably would only be scolded for acting so foolishly. All muddy, head to toe, I got up about a hundred meters from the trucks parked in front of the factory. No one noticed I was there. The trucks came aboard Kazakh ships, but there were no trucks from Hungary as I'd expect with the rich Hungarian soil to help us cultivate luscious grapes for the future vineyard.

Stealthily, like a cat ready to hunt its prey, shoulders up, tail down, I crawled under one of the trucks. Two men stood in front of the truck speaking Russian. They were called in by other men in the factory. "Break is over," a Cuban man said with an accent clearly from the easternmost part of the island.

The lights in the factory were on, yet there was no smoke coming from the smokestacks or any toxic smells coming from inside. Not that I knew what creating a vineyard would entail, but I expected some signs of production instead of just men and trucks standing around.

On my back, I pulled myself out from under the Kazakh truck. There must be petroleum cans inside, I thought; these trucks always carry some sort of combustible fluid. After pulling open the tarp that covered the back, all I saw was wet, rich soil. No cans, no petroleum.

As I was about to exit the truck, my foot sank in the muddy soil inside. There was something under my foot, packages of some sort. After yanking my foot out of the thick soil, I noticed my shoe was covered with a white powder. The

98

mediciny smell told me it must've been nitrates and all that stuff that the guards said needed to be infused into our soil.

I couldn't go back empty-handed. Nestor would undoubtedly succeed in getting the necessary supplies, and how would that make me look? Maybe if I just snuck a peek inside the factory. Yeah, I could say I got lost or something if someone found me. In any case, I was sure to be bombarded with questions from my *compañeros* as to what was going on in here. It was my duty as their comrade out on the field to bring back some information to satiate their curiosity.

The factory was split into two distinct sections. One side looked like a dark truck stop where not a sound was heard except for the snoring of two guards who stood at the back of the loading dock, their chins resting on their nuzzles to keep themselves from falling over. The other side was a brightly-lit laboratory with workers running up and down, oblivious of the dimly lit side. It was one giant mandala, one side night the other day.

Unlike the trucks I saw going into the factory, these were gargantuan. There was Cyrillic writing on them; the only part clear to me was the large bold red letters that read WARNING FISSILE MATERIALS. There was hardly anyone on that side of the factory. Tired after a long transatlantic journey, the trucks seemed to sleep regardless of the activity taking place on the other side. The large Kazakh trucks, which looked more like eighteen-wheeler armored tanks than anything else, were lined up to head out the back of the factory where the sleeping guards found their respite.

The other half of the factory was lit and running. And this part was further split into two stories, most of the action happening on the bottom floor. There were workers wearing surgical masks, and they carried packages of what looked like the same powder I stepped in from one conveyor belt to another. No guards asleep there. High-volume boiling vats with hoses let out smoke; they looked like the vats the *guajiros* kept on their farms to make rum or *aguardiente*.

Following one of the hoses, I noticed they all exited the same side of the factory and went under water, right beyond the

99

shore. No wonder there was no smoke, no odor, no signs of work when viewed from outside. Why were they being so crafty in making sure the smoke went underwater? Maybe it had something to do with the environment.

The workers sifted through this white powder with gloves. I went down onto the actual floor where they were working. Hiding behind crates that held six bottles of clear syrup, I held my breath so as not to make a sound. What in the world were they doing? Like drones, the laborers just grabbed crates and bottles, took them to the vats, and mixed the white powder with the proper ingredients as carefully as when my mother tried one time to make a soufflé. I had never heard of such a thing for soil. Then again, we did have a new Agricultural Minister. God knows what she was implementing to impress the higher-ups.

Two Cubans in their faded avocado fatigues were coming down to where I crouched. *Mierda*, how did I get myself into this? At this point, I forgot about the petroleum for Albertico's leg and just closed my eyes hoping they wouldn't see me. They were smoking cigars and mumbling about the trucks from Kazakhstan on the other side of the factory and how uneasy this made them. There was room between the crates of acetone for me to sneak in and stay there until the coast was clear.

"*Oye, cuida'o con eso,*" warned one of the uniformed men to a clumsy worker who dropped the powder on the floor.

"You think this stuff is cheap?" roared his superior who spoke with a funny Spanish accent.

The drone was obviously shaken up and scooped what he could off the floor. The rest was swept up into a drain in the middle of the room, the kind of drain I once saw in a mortuary when Nestor and I sneaked in to see what a live dead body looked like. We had nightmares for three days straight after that!

"*¡Atención!*" I heard from the top floor. I looked up and everyone worked faster and faster, moving several of the bottles at a time, and some people were shaking the hoses to assure the smoke would continue flowing efficiently out to sea.

I couldn't believe it. Raúl, the President's brother himself, stepped into the room! He looked just like his brother,

100

except shorter and rounder. His army fatigues were muddy but not faded like the rest of the soldiers, and his boots left tracks everywhere he turned. I have to admit I was star-struck.

"*Comandante,*" an officer saluted, dropping his rifle like a nervous schoolboy dropping his books.

"Not the *Comandante* yet. Wait until the world finds out the green mango has withered away, then I'm the *Comandante* - officially," Raúl scoffed.

Everyone laughed at our President's expense. Even his own brother joked about the green mango who would fall off the proverbial tree. But why did he say when the world finds out he has withered away?

A Russian man greeted him and gesticulated this way and that like a great orator, no doubt explaining, with the utmost respect, the current operations. At one point, they all laughed and passed more cigars around. Raúl Castro's eyes were on fire. His cheeks were rosy, not the usual sallow complexion I saw in many pictures. I needed to get out of there. They certainly couldn't stand there forever. As soon as the opportunity presented itself, I would haul ass out of there, head up the hill and tell everyone what was going on, even though I myself wasn't quite sure.

"*¿Qué tal?*" I heard in a familiar American accent. Lo and behold, when I looked through the side of the crates, there was Mr. Mendelsen, my stepfather's friend. There was no forgetting that awful "*Kay tall.*"

Raúl hugged him and the proper introductions were done all around. Raúl hugging an American? What were all those speeches about "*muerte a todos los yanquis*"? Maybe he didn't know Mr. Mendelsen was American, but how could he not with that thick accent Cubans pretend to find endearing?

Raúl picked up a mirrored tray, brought to him by one of the drones, which held samples of the white powder. He touched a little to his tongue. What in the world was going on?

Raúl passed the tray around, but Mr. Mendelsen refused, "*Tengo problemas con mis senos.*"

"*¿Tus senos?*" one of the workers exclaimed. Everyone laughed as the word for "sinus" and "breast" is the same in

101

Spanish, and the way Mr. Mendelsen worded it, it sounded as if he said he was having "problems with his breasts." It took a lot for me not to give myself away by snickering along with the rest of them, but I controlled myself.

No one insisted for the American with breast problems to snort some powder. Everyone just smacked him on the back, pointed to his chest, and laughed. Mr. Mendelsen grew nervous, not knowing what he had said or why everyone pointed to his chest. He was sweating more and more, cheeks flushed like the night he killed my siren, my princess, Zyrena.

This was too surreal. Maybe the smell of the chemicals in the factory was getting to me. Perhaps it was an hallucination. They were snorting drugs right there in front of me, knowing what poison this was to the masses, knowing the Marxist jihad against drugs that Castro spoke about all the time when criticizing our American neighbors.

Was it my duty to yell out from where I stood and warn my countrymen that Mr. Mendelsen murdered Zyrena at the Marina Hemingway or that he was in cahoots with my stepfather, bombing parts of our island to terrorize our nation? I would be a hero like my father for sure, probably a martyr as they'd shoot me the minute I yelled out from behind the crates. Then I remembered what Fortuna told me. Sometimes it is important just to be still.

"This is more than I ever anticipated," Raúl stated. "Make sure you don't mix it too much. I want it to be as pure as possible."

"It'll still be Grade A, almost as pure as the Colombian stuff, but we're also tripling its yield," assured Mr. Mendelsen. I never heard Mr. Mendelsen speak Spanish again.

"*Bueno, bueno*," grinned our President's brother, Raúl, "You Americans are sneaky. I don't know how you're tripling it, but this will make the Pan-American Games an experience foreigners will never forget. Come to Cuba, see wonderful sights, enjoy our pretty *señoritas*, and snort the best *yeyo* in the Caribbean."

Everyone laughed at the heir-apparent's wit. Two men patted the bearded one on the back, parroting each other how

102

they themselves would have never thought up such a strategy for revitalizing the economy and keeping foreigners coming back for more.

"How many kilos can we smuggle to your country, Señor Mendelsen?" Raúl asked with his beard pointing straight out, blowing smoke rings into the *yanqui's* face. "Needless to say, there's only so much I can keep here."

"Smuggle sounds like such a bad thing," the American answered. Everyone laughed. "But we'll take as much as you can spare, Mr. President, I mean Mr. Vice-President." Everyone laughed again. What was so funny? Why were people making jokes about Raúl being the President?

Then, more seriously, Raúl stated, "Then it's settled."

"Now, being Grade A, tripling its yield or not, it's still going to cost you."

"As long as it's straight from the truck, I think my people are still comfortable with our agreement. Leave all that cutting and mixing to us," Mr. Mendelsen said, a prudent businessman he was.

"We've received more than anticipated," an officer stated with his eyes down, awaiting the Vice-President's permission to continue speaking.

"You may have three truckloads instead of the original two," Raúl agreed, "at the original price per kilo. The Colombians seemed to overdo it this time. You get it out of here any way you can. My side's taken care of. You won't have any problems leaving the country. But you've got your American Coast Guard to worry about. That's not my problem, you understand."

"Understood," Mendelsen smiled, shaking on it with Raúl and the rest of the men who were now so proud to be part of such an historic moment that I could tell it hurt them just to stand still.

I stumbled into something that just didn't make sense. Why was our Vice-President, *El Líder's* own brother, wheeling and dealing with an American, a *gusano* who was part of the Omega Underground? This, I'm sure, the President's brother

103

didn't know. Otherwise, we'd be bombing our own island. Made no sense.

Why were drugs coming into our island? Why would Castro want to deal it on our own island and sell the surplus to the USA? Moreover, why would the Americans be buying that stuff from us? So often we criticized the drug-addicted Americans for their lax stance on drugs. We'd see videos of people shooting up in the streets. This was a government ploy, we were told, to keep the lower class in their proper caste or to spread AIDS amongst the users as a covert form of genocide.

Maybe this is what Lenin and Marx meant by material dialectics, a term most of my generation didn't comprehend but, nevertheless, we heard it used whenever people didn't understand the dichotomy of a current Cuban crisis. Dialectics or no dialectics, there was nothing right about this.

Most people remember the moment their lives change forever; this was mine. I thought seeing Zyrena being killed and the marina being blown up changed my life forever, but that would fade over time; this wouldn't. Disillusionment shrouded me like a cocoon, ripping off my blinders just like those of the mares in my dreams.

I could hear Fortuna repeating her mantra that this was a blessing, sacred. My cheeks flushed with warm blood, and my stomach quivered with nausea as the reality I once knew metamorphosed into the blinding actuality that I could no longer live on this island, could no longer feel at home here.

I'm sure my father, may he rest in peace, would have been changed, too, if he were able to experience what I just did firsthand. Perhaps he would be alive today if he knew the charade of the philosophical masks that caused him to die in Angola. What a waste of a life.

Seeing the coast was clear, I went back to camp. Nestor was right; I think too much. That was the longest walk back. I tried to focus on what I'd tell everybody. I had to be careful as I didn't know who would turn me in or call me a traitor for making up such a fantastic story. But my leaders had proven already to be traitors themselves. Nothing could hurt me more.

Fortuna once told me to keep my eyes always on God, never on men. "Men will disappoint you, deceive you, even destroy you," she'd say. By keeping her eyes in the heavens, Fortuna had peace, contentment, and wisdom. She had faced illusion and waved it away with her hands, living a life many of us didn't understand. But I think I understood her now. I had so much to learn, and I wished she were here to console me.

CHAPTER 12

The night was clearing up. A few lightning bolts here and there still struck the island to remind us that the weather had not made up its mind as to which way it would turn. It reminded me that *Changó* was probably still fighting with the rest of the *Orísha* like Fortuna had said.

I came back as drenched as I had left the camp. Albertico was lying in bed, asleep. Nestor had given him a clonazepam he smuggled out of the camp clinic to calm him down. They said the guards heard all the screaming and crying and thought we were beating up Albertico.

"Dumb little shit," I mumbled.

"Where's the petrol?" my cousin asked. "I got needles, aspirin, you name it. That witch of a nurse was so drunk. She had someone hiding in there with her. I think I interrupted her and one of the guards. But I pretended not to notice, even though the place smelled like alcohol and sweat! She gave me anything I asked for, didn't even ask what the needle was for. She just wanted me out of there and quick. Man, that's luck!" Nestor was beside himself.

"I couldn't get the petroleum."

"You couldn't even get any tar from the shore?" my cousin asked, eyebrows furrowing into his eye sockets.

"What the hell took you so long, then?" *Jirafa* accused. *"¡Le zumba el merequetén!"*

I sneered at him, waiting for another word out of his mouth so I could just ring his long, skinny neck.

"He was probably out there with the Vietnamese magazine," *El Bizco* said. Everyone giggled.

"You're gonna go blind," *El Morito* said from the back bunk.

"You could go blind from that?" *El Bizco* asked as he gulped. Everyone roared with laughter again.

"Just shut up, all right? I'm not in the mood!"

"¿Oye, qué te pica, acere?" Nestor asked me. "Don't worry about it, we'll use mud. It's all the same."

I didn't say another word that evening. I didn't know where to begin. I just lay on my bunk staring at the stains on the underside of the mattress above me. Like clouds, these stains took on different shapes in my mind. I felt the red and black *eleke* beads I managed to salvage from the bus, loose in my pocket, praying to *los santos* for guidance.

The boys rattled on all night about what they should do to Albertico to assure he'd be sent home the next day. Everyone was afraid of needles and wouldn't dare inject him with mud or kerosene. They passed the needle around, but everyone became nauseated at the thought of feeling the needle hit bone or feeling it wiggle around in Albertico's foot.

"Just break his foot," *El Enamora'o* offered. "He's asleep and will probably be knocked out for the rest of the night from what you gave him, Nestor."

"He took the sedative willingly," Nestor quickly retorted. *"¡No me echen el muerto, ahora!"*

"What about if he never wakes up?" *El Enamora'o* asked.

"Of course he'll wake up. Just shut up," Nestor defended his actions. "You're all a bunch of little girls."

They grabbed part of Albertico's sheet and wet it with some rainwater dripping from the doorframe. Taking his limp leg, I heard them wrapping Albertico's foot so it would be nice and clammy by morning.

They all chickened out and threw away the needle. It was better this way. I was relieved to hear that they were sticking to a sure-fire remedy that had been perfected years ago, years before we were born. They'd take the bunk in the morning, *uno, dos y tres*, and wham, Albertico's foot or ankle, depending on

107

the aim, would shatter. This was much safer for everybody involved.

The boys sat around, playing cards, smoking cigarettes, trying to work the TV antenna to get some type of reception. They were hoping to find something else besides the Russian cartoons that incessantly played on Channel 3. Some of them counted the lapse between the thunder and lightning, betting on when the next storm would hit us. None of this mattered to me.

Finally, after manipulating the antenna and changing the black-and-white's position around the room, my comrades managed to get WCIX Channel 6 from Miami. They roared with excitement at not only deafening those wretched Russian cartoons but at reaching out across the sea and grabbing hold of real *yanqui* television.

I heard commercials playing and almost everyone in the barracks could follow what was being said – except for colloquialisms, which always mystified us no matter how good our English became. I had to look, so I rolled over, hugging my musty pillow and saw my first *yanqui* commercial. I felt like some peeping Tom, sneaking a peek into the minds of North American capitalists. I wondered if my relatives in Miami were watching the same exact channel right now. I wondered if they wondered what I was doing.

The commercial was for a store named Burdines. They seemed to carry everything you could possibly ever want, and all at 50% off that week! Shoes. Designer clothes. TVs. There was some sort of Clearance Sale. Nestor explained to the troupe that this was the American way. When fashions got out of style, the stores let you know by giving it all away at half off.

Jirafa said that his family in Miami sent him clothes from Burdines all the time. He sold it in the black market in exchange for food and US dollars. His family was able to eat for a whole month on a pair of Levi's, Nike's, and a T-shirt that changed colors from purple to green to fuchsia due to some sort of heat-sensitive cotton. Americans think of everything! But his family back in Miami didn't know he hocked their stuff. They'd be hurt and would stop sending gifts. I'm sure if he explained it to them they'd understand that we needed a loaf of bread or a

108

gram of coffee or rice much more than a pair of tennis shoes with a built-in air pump.

The model on TV spoke with a rich un-American accent, lisping due to a gap in her front teeth that made her even more alluring. Although we couldn't understand most of what she was saying, she was better than any Vietnamese rag any day! Everyone grew quiet. The model, who later identified herself as Lauren something-or-other, was then rolling around on a haystack, playing with other girls as the Burdines logo danced all around them like an out-of-control ball of fire.

We didn't care what they were selling, but oh, how we all wished to have whatever it was she was giving away at half off. The commercial's reggae music and pictures of beautifully built men and women strolling around what I would later know as South Beach made us all envious of life less than 150 km away. The TV screen went gray with a loud SHHH, and someone turned it off.

"Everyone looks so happy in Miami," *El Bizco* muttered, his eyes twitching nervously after witnessing such splendor.

"It's all just a ploy," interjected *El Enamora'o*. "They base happiness on material objects. I don't know how they can live like that. But that's what keeps them going."

"What do you know?" Nestor challenged. "They all look pretty satisfied to me."

Nestor had the last word. Everybody just turned to their bunks and went to sleep, no doubt dreaming of Lauren, the slender gap-toothed model, and of all the riches America offered.

I now understood why so many of my comrades fled generations ago to the U.S. I understood why so many of those who stayed called them *gusanos,* worms. We were jealous that we didn't have the *cojones* to turn our backs on chimerical philosophies that rang of truth and justice, to admit that what had been so bloody, so passionate, was for naught. We replaced one extremist group with another as if the opposite side of the spectrum, the pushing of the political pendulum from right to left, would annul our pain.

The rapping rain on the tin roof put me to sleep. I had seen too much, witnessed too much. I dreamed of the mares at

109

Lenin Park. Brushing their gray and chestnut coats, I told them everything would be all right, and I didn't feel guilty about lying. Their salt and pepper hair follicles fell to the ground without their knowing. "It'll be OK," I lied to them in my sleep. "You'll be just fine."

I ignored *La Virgen de Regla, Yemayá* herself, who watched me consoling the mares. I just wanted to make sure the inclement weather didn't blow away their blinders. That would be dreadful.

CHAPTER 13

The next morning I awoke to Albertico's screaming. Everyone was trying to muffle his cries. God knows the guards had had it with us taunting this poor boy.

"You rather have the injection?" my cousin warned as if speaking to a four-year-old.

"Just get it over with already!" Albertico cried.

"*¡Uno, dos y tres!*" Slam! The bunk fell on the child's saturated foot, and *crunch* the deed was done.

Everyone cheered and shook hands, lighting cigarettes as if a major task had just been completed, which it had. Albertico's face was identical to a painting I once saw called *The Scream*. Identical! There was no voice, no sound, just a giant silent scream. It was the loudest scream I never heard.

The guards came in, tramping through the rain, and took Albertico away. He was sent home. The job was done. These idiots fell for it every time. Albertico had a limp for a while, I heard, but he never had to go back to do *trabajo voluntario*.

The guards advised us that morning that we weren't going to have plumbing for awhile. This meant using the abandoned outhouses, which were crawling with tropical tarantulas and non-poisonous, tan-colored snakes with a pale neck band. Although both these tarantulas and snakes were no threat to humans, as all snakes in Cuba are non-poisonous, both these critters' bites were aggressive and unforgiving.

No plumbing also meant bathing outside before it stopped raining. Most of us didn't use the outhouses during the rains anyway, not because of the snakes and spiders, but because these always overflowed when too much rain came.

111

Everyone grabbed whatever they could to use as soap or shampoo. Nestor and I used what was left of the soap we couldn't sell to our troupe. Being stuck in our barracks for days now, the thought of running around naked in the woods made us elated. Besides, the barracks reeked of underarms and farts. It was time for a bath! We were very thankful! They were allowing us – no, commanding us – to run around naked in the rain, slipping and sliding in mud, peeing behind trees. It really couldn't get any better than this.

El Morito somersaulted straight into the mud, knocking down three boys who were standing there like bowling pins.

Jirafa extended his long neck upward to drink in the falling rain. He beat his chest when his mouth was full and spit it out on whoever was closest. After we bathed, Nestor and I put our arms together to create a swing, letting our comrades sit on our arms as we rocked back and forth and flung them into the mud.

A few of us even began doing a conga line *A-e, A-e, A-e la chambelona* – kick.

I forgot all about last night's adventure at the factory, Raúl Castro, last night's Burdine's commercial, and I just frolicked innocently, laughing at how we of Troupe No. 476 all looked like natives running around with mud in our every orifice. After about an hour of this horseplay, the guards looking on entertained, we all reached for the saturated palm fronds to help us sponge off the mud. I had mud under my nails, in my ears, even up my nostrils. But we were clean and had fun doing it! This was better than the Jet Skis at the Marina Hemingway any day.

"Hey," my cousin nudged. "Look at all them trucks leaving the factory." He pointed to the armored trucks with the red bold FISSILE MATERIALS on them. Their slumber was over and now they were heading east.

"Let's go investigate," he insisted, eyes wide open.

"C'mon, Nestor, there's nothing there to investigate," I urged.

"¡Qué pendejo, acere!"

"Maybe later, OK?"

112

"Fine, but don't think you're getting out of this one. You came back awfully quiet last night. And I know that only means one thing. You saw something you didn't want me to see. You saw something you're going to pretend isn't real."

My cousin was more astute than I gave him credit for being.

"Tonight's the night," he promised and then joined the wet, naked conga-liners – *A-e, a-e, a-e la chambelona!*

CHAPTER 14

The winds grew more aggressive, buffeting the sides of the barracks and forcing trees to bend at their fulcrum point, almost snapping them in half. No one had ever heard thunder like this before. *Changó* must've really been at it! The radio said that water was even coming over the *malecón*. Well, the clamoring and thunderbolts shook the guards to such an extent that they came around with candles and apples as an offering to appease *Changó*. Although these apples tantalized us, we knew we couldn't eat fruit offered to the gods – well, not all of them.

I was relieved as there was no way Nestor could make me go down to the factory in this weather.

"*¿Y la baraja?*" I asked, as the deck of cards was nowhere to be found, and I was in the mood for some canasta.

"Forget about that, we got work to do," my cousin nodded furtively.

"Nestor, are you crazy or what? How are we supposed to go through that rain? Listen to that wind! Didn't you just hear on the radio that waves were even going over the breakwater?"

"Waves aren't going over the *malecón*. You know how those Cuban broadcasters are; they embellish everything to make it sound better."

He was right. If the broadcasters didn't make it sound good, people complained. If people complained, the broadcasters were assigned another job. That's just the way it was in my country. We didn't just care about the facts; we wanted drama!

Jirafa stretched his rubber-like neck out of the bunk, barely having to move most of his torso. "Where you going?"

"Yeah, where you going?" asked all my bored comrades in unison.

"Nowhere. We're not going anywhere," I asserted. "Nestor has these crazy ideas."

"If you don't come with me, I'll go alone," my cousin threatened.

"All right," I conceded, "but if you get struck by a thunderbolt or something, don't think I'm going to drag your sorry ass back here."

"Where you going?" *El Bizco* insisted, eyes whacked out of alignment.

"Nowhere," my cousin and I both answered.

"Don't be such a *chismosa*," I added.

"I'm not nosy; just want to know what's up?"

"Look," my cousin whispered to the whole group who huddled in closer expecting one of Nestor's tall tales, "we just want to go down to the factory – see what's up. That's all."

Everyone shouted and begged Nestor and me to let them come with us. But we convinced them that they were just kids and needed to stay safe from the storm, even though some of them were a couple years older than we were. We promised them that if we needed their help, one of us would fire a flare. And their job was to stand by the window and look for that flare. No one even asked where in the world we got hold of a flare gun. It was the drama of it all.

"Yeah, yeah," agreed *El Codo*. "I'll be on the first watch with…you and then…you here." They began forming teams of four guards per team. The barracks vibrated with the excitement of forming teams and handing out duties and ranks. Kids raised their hands to be picked on the first team (no one wanted to be picked last), and Nestor and I sneaked out during the titillation.

We ventured out into the storm, the first group of watchers standing guard by the window, in case we shot the flare on their watch. Going behind the adult barracks near *Bloque No. 18* and down the hill, I tried not to think of what they'd do to us if they found us. Look at what happened to *El Poeta* just for speaking his mind. My cousin stopped me and pointed to the trucks that seemed to be endlessly going in and out of the

115

factory, even during the storm. They must've been on a tight schedule or needed to bring in a certain number before morning. Running even faster, his curiosity beating logic, Nestor slid, hurdled over fallen branches, and dragged me along with him.

"Easy, *acere*!"

"C'mon!" is all Nestor said. "C'mon!"

We arrived at the factory in what seemed like seconds. There were men putting sandbags around the back of the factory where the loading dock and another entrance was. It wasn't just high tide; waves were beating the side of the factory and were merciless thrashing against the men with sandbags who were trying to protect the trucks and workers taking refuge against the elements. I never saw the ocean so angry.

Almost everyone was outside trying to protect the factory, like black knights protecting an evil fortress. Visibility was almost nil as the rain beat our faces. We stood behind one of the parked trucks, the ones with the drugs, and my cousin pointed at the light blue, black, yellow and gold Kazakh crest on the doors. Acting as surprised as he was, I nodded as if saying, *I can't believe it*. The trucks continued coming, though. In and out. In and out.

I could see Nestor's intention. He wanted to jump on one of the trucks so that we could hitch a ride into the factory.

"No, Nestor."

"No, what?" he said as he grabbed me by my T-shirt.

"I know what you're thinking. We can't jump on these trucks."

"It's the only way in," Nestor urged, his eyes blinking away the pounding rain.

"No, we'll come back tomorrow or something. When there aren't so many men outside."

"What you scared of? We've done this hundreds of times." My cousin was referring to how often we jumped on the back of buses with our friends to hitch a free ride to wherever they were giving away plantains or rice. We could do it with our eyes closed, that's how good we were. But this was different.

"*Uno*," Nestor began counting the trucks.

"No, we can't."

116

"*Dos.*"

"Look, we'll get killed."

"*Y tres!*" Before I knew it, my feet were off the ground and I was hanging onto a moving truck with my cousin.

"Go inside," I gesticulated so the next truck coming up behind us wouldn't see two kids hanging on the back.

We fell inside onto the wet soil.

"See, just soil for the vineyards," I pointed out.

"Yeah, and what's this?" Nestor held out a bag of white powder.

I was hoping to find nothing so that my cousin's curiosity wouldn't jolt him any further. But instead, he found Kazakh trucks, drugs…there was no getting out of this one. The truck pulled into the factory near where I hid the day before. It moved onto a platform next to a colossal canister where the soil was being dumped to separate the kilos from the camouflaging soil.

Both parts of the factory were awake this evening, not just the laboratory. We could hear people shouting at one of the drivers of the armored trucks who almost drove the eighteen-wheeler, along with all the fissile materials, right off the loading dock. It wasn't his fault, he said, he had never driven such a huge truck like this before.

"We gotta get outta here!" I warned, afraid that we would be pushed out into the bin where the men with the white coats and surgical masks were sifting. Afraid our island and half of this planet would soon blow up if these inexperienced drivers simply pressed the wrong gadget or pedal. I knew these trucks carried drugs, but I didn't like the looks of the way the letters FISSILE MATERIALS were juxtaposed. Maybe it was the red color; maybe it was the stern looking font.

"Just hang on to the side," Nestor whispered, grabbing on to the frame of the inside of the truck.

"Let's just tell them we got lost," I began to say as the back of the truck started to elevate away from the cabin!

"Oh, shit!" Nestor yelled. The men looked around, but didn't know who had shouted. It could've been anyone, really.

117

"Just hold on," I whispered as the trailer continued elevating.

Nestor and I hung on to opposite sides of the truck, hoping the rotting wooden planks framing the trailer wouldn't give way. All the soil began to slide out from the truck as we continued to hang onto the frame that creaked with our weight. If anyone came inside to shovel the remaining dirt out, we were dead for sure. The back of the truck was now perfectly vertical, all its contents poured onto the giant bin where men grabbed packages and threw them onto an adjacent conveyor belt.

Just as I began to lose my grip, seeing my cousin's triceps trembling from the exertion, the back of the truck began to take its original horizontal position. We heard the men tell the drivers to get the shovels in case any packages stayed stuck inside. There was no time to lose.

I froze in place knowing we were going to be discovered, my brain filling with excuses as to why we were there. Seeing that the drivers got out, though, Nestor opened the false canvas back of the cabin and squirmed his way into the driver's seat. Without another thought, I inched my way into the passenger side, which smelled like onions, and rested my head on the inside of the passenger door.

"What do we do?" I whispered to Nestor who acted as if I weren't even there. His brain was reeling as fast as mine. The men came onto the back of the truck and began shoveling the rest of the mud looking for leftover kilos.

"Clean!" one of them said as they both jumped back out and closed the tarp.

Knowing the drivers would surely return into the cabin after shoveling the surplus dirt, in order to move the truck to make room for the other ones on the platform, Nestor and I found our way back into the now-empty trailer and closed the false back that separated the cabin and the trailer.

We felt the truck move and didn't say a word. I closed my eyes, stomach pounding with nervous energy, my heart beating in my ears.

"C'mon," my cousin whispered, leading me away from the partition. "We gotta get outta here."

118

"Of course, we gotta get outta here," I agreed, hating Nestor for getting me yet into another crisis. Fortuna's warnings rang in my ears. She warned me to go with my instincts, and I certainly didn't this time.

The truck drove away from the platform and outside the factory where it remained parked. We heard the drivers jump out, happy their shift was over. Not knowing what to do or where to go, we just sat in the back of the truck gasping for air, wishing this was all a bad dream.

"Let's go," Nestor urged.

"Where?"

"We can't stay here. C'mon the coast is clear now. It's now or never."

We slid out of the rear looking at the workers inside the factory empty more trucks. Guards stood in a line to ensure that these trucks headed into the laboratory and didn't collide with the armored Kazakh trucks. I could tell Nestor was trying to figure out what was happening, the same look he always framed on his face when our math teacher asked him to solve a word problem. I didn't have the energy or courage to explain what I had seen the night before, so I began to traipse my way back into the woods when Nestor grabbed me by the nape of my neck.

"Where you going?"

"Back to the camp. Haven't you had enough? We could've been killed."

"You don't even care one little bit what's happening here?"

"I already know. C'mon and I'll explain." I had him hooked.

We scurried into the edge of the woods outside the factory and I explained all I saw the night before. I told him about Raúl Castro, Mr. Mendelsen, the deal they were discussing, the drugs, and the armored trucks from Kazakhstan carrying fissile materials. I was even detailed enough to tell him of the two guards who slept by the loading dock and how everyone kept saying Fidel Castro had already withered away.

He made me repeat the events to him three times, testing my consistency. It was obvious he didn't believe what I was

119

saying and was trying to find some hole in my story, some gap in my plot that would force us back so he could conduct a proper investigation. But I just told him the facts – no embellishments, no rising action, no climax. I even told him about the picture I saw back at the Marina Hemingway when Zyrena was murdered.

I explained the theories I had about my stepfather and Mr. Mendelsen, but what I couldn't explain was why Raúl was in cahoots with the Omega Underground.

"He's not," Nestor assured me.

"How do you know?"

"It wouldn't make sense."

"None of this makes any sense, why should *that*?" I asked, the winds and rain fiercely pounding us where we sat.

"I could see that they're dealing drugs. Who cares about that," Nestor said. "*El Comandante* would do anything to bring us money."

"You mean to bring *him* money."

"Whatever, what I'm saying is that they must not know that Mr. Mendelsen is part of the Omega Underground. He's double crossing him. Those North Americans are smart *hijos de puta*. They're wheeling and dealing with the President's brother to give them a reason to be on this island. Don't you see?"

No. I didn't see at all. I didn't care at all. I just wanted to go back to camp and forget what I experienced these past few weeks. I was going to make myself believe that I saw nothing, heard nothing, and would live the rest of my life that way.

Nestor pushed me against the Cuban oak that withstood many storms. The tree didn't even flinch a branch at my pounding it with my back or at the storm trying to exfoliate its wet bark and foliage.

"Are you listening to me?" my cousin pushed again.

"Yes," I pushed back, "now can we go back to camp?"

"No, we gotta go back inside the factory and see if we can find any proof we could take back with us."

"That's it," I stood up, resolute that I had had enough. "I'm going back and you can do whatever the hell you want, but just don't get me involved in any of this. You're gonna get yourself killed, Nestor!"

"You're the one who's always talking about duty, responsibility and all that bullshit you believe in. Wasn't it you who said it was wrong for us to even go to the marina? Now here you are telling me..."

"Just shut up! Shut up!" I couldn't bear hearing my words thrown in my face, especially since I had abandoned any feeling of patriotism, camaraderie, or any principle concerning Cuba's current state of affairs. It was all a lie. The democratic socialism I believed in was a lie, everything I ever learned and knew to be true was a lie, and I would no longer be part of any of this.

"Were there any offices or desks or files – anything at all when you were in there?" my cousin probed.

"*No sé.* I just saw a bunch of workers and everyone was walking around. There were crates and stuff, which I hid behind."

"Then we gotta go look. We need proof, that's all there is to it."

Once again, we crawled out of the woods, away from the Cuban oak under which we huddled, and we sneaked into the factory. My cousin promised that we'd be out of there before I knew it. We were on a search-and-rescue mission. Our goal: go in, find proof, head for camp. If only things were as easy as Nestor made them out to be. My life could've turned out totally different.

CHAPTER 15

I led Nestor to the crates behind where I hid the night before. Most of the men were either by the trucks on the other side of the factory or outside by the shore, still battling the waves that threatened the building and their radioactive trucks. We looked around trying to find anything we could render as evidence. Render to whom I didn't know, because if Raúl himself was here, el Comandante's brother, to whom were we going to give this evidence?

There were two sets of metal stairs on opposite sides of the factory which didn't look very sturdy by the way they shook and rattled when someone used them to go up to the office or come down to the plant floor. Parts of these steps were ulcerated with rust. Nestor thought this was due to the salt air. I pointed to Nestor where I saw the President's brother with Mr. Mendelsen at the top of the stairs overlooking the vats, workers, and trucks.

"We gotta go up there," Nestor instructed with his eyes wide open as if calling me un comemierda. He continued, "We have no choice in the matter. Perhaps they dropped something, a note, a phone number, something."

It was clear my cousin and I had seen too many detective movies at El Cine Yara. Tattered screen and all, the movies we saw there were quite effective in filling our heads with fantasies that only manifested into trouble. As we were about to make our way to the metal stairs closest to us, the lights in the factory began to blink. The air was filled with the buzz of machinery gasping to stay on.

We waited, watching people scurry like an army of unfocused ants that lost their way home, ants that were

122

threatened by tropical tarantulas or tan-colored snakes. The generators soon answered the call of duty and spotlights came on in various essential places of the factory. The speaker nearest to us just buzzed and clicked, clearly needing repair, but the clicking and buzzing sounded urgent. We continued walking toward the metal stairs, the confusion in *la fábrica* actually keeping us invisible.

The last time Nestor and I were sneaking around like this, we saw Zyrena get murdered and my world was turned upside down. What could possibly happen this time that would be more sensational, more unnerving than that? More unnerving than last night's histrionics? Couldn't be. This thought calmed me for a few seconds. Just couldn't get any worse.

Once atop, the metal platform creaking where the rusted bolts fused the frame into the concrete, we rushed across hoping the chaos below would continue hiding us like the teenage fugitives we were. There wasn't much need for this area except for overseeing the progress of both sides of the factory, the laboratory, and the garage.

This section reminded me of pictures of the tobacco factories in the old days, which all had small platforms like this one to oversee the workers, many of whom were women, rolling the cigars. On those platforms sat *lectores* who read to the workers to pass the time. Perhaps they read some of Martí's poetry or perhaps some of Lima's memorable quotes. Workers were kept quiet, produced more than in factories that didn't have "readers," and they never dared to put any tobacco leaves in their pockets or purses.

This didn't remind Nestor of anything; he was as focused as ever. He just hoped that, like in the movies, they'd keep an office with file cabinets and paperwork up here. And how his face lit up when his hopes were realized. Hollywood hadn't let him down yet.

"¿Qué te dije?" Nestor rubbed in my face. "I told you they'd have an office or something. They always do. That's why you always see people (he meant in the movies) shredding papers, and burning file cabinets, and all...you know." He

123

couldn't contain his glee. "We're going to take evidence and make them pay for this, Uli!"

"What? Am I hearing you right? You said we were just here for proof. You didn't say anything about making anybody pay. You think a couple of teenagers can blackmail the President successfully? They'll kill you, Nestor. This ain't a movie. People get shot just for mouthing off. Look what happened to *El Poeta*. You think they'll let us live if they find out that we know about the drugs or about the fissile material? *Estás más loco que una cabra.*"

"The way things are going? They wouldn't touch us! With the Omega Underground blowing up parts of the island, Mr. Mendelsen, the drug dealing, they'll pay to shut us up."

"You're crazy!"

"I'll be living at the Marina Hemingway for the rest of my life!" my cousin wishfully thought aloud. "Or even Miami and shopping at Burdines!"

"Grab a hold of yourself," I warned my cousin who was drunk with one delusional plausibility after another. But I realized the imminent danger we were in. We still needed to get out of here and back to the camp in one piece. So I wasn't going to argue anymore with Nestor. Common sense told me to agree with anything he said and get out of there.

We rummaged through the files and saw receipts in English, Spanish, Chinese, and in Cyrillic writing. There were files authenticating the factory as an agricultural project for the future vineyard and signature stamps of all sorts – not one I recognized. My heart raced trying to figure out what was important and what papers were mere trivialities of the Cuban government, mere lies.

"Aha!" my cousin shouted, forgetting where we were.

"*Coño*, keep it down. What did you find?"

Picking up a picture of someone laying in a coffin, "Who does this look like to you?"

It couldn't be. There was an entire file, which at first I was convinced must've been fabricated, documenting the President's death, dated 1991. Fidel Castro dead? No way. We would have heard about it by now. The Cuban government ain't

124

that smart to keep something like this under wraps for a full year. In fact, we still heard his speeches on the radio and saw him on TV.

"He's dead, Uli! The green mango finally fell off the tree!" My cousin's happiness was contagious. Not happy at the actual fact that Fidel was dead, but the fact that we knew something most of the world didn't.

"*No puerde ser*," I said, trying to sober him up. "Don't you think someone would have found out by now? Who's been running the country? As power hungry as Raúl is, don't you think he would've let the world know immediately that he was now our President?"

"Not if the rest of the world wasn't ready," Nestor responded slowly, making it up as he went along.

My cousin didn't know it, but there was a lot of wisdom in that one sentence. What if the world wasn't ready to have their shades taken away? What if the Americans, through Mr. Mendelsen and others, weren't ready for us to tell the world that after all these years it was finally over. Perhaps all their deals weren't complete, and they were afraid that too many eyes would be focused on our island once again, divulging their secrets. What if Raúl had something up his sleeve, a reason to stay in the background with the power and the money? Maybe he was smarter than we and the world gave him credit.

"Let me see the picture," I asked as my cousin kept reading the documents in the manila folder.

"It's true, Uli. It's all here," my cousin mumbled as I grabbed hold of one of a dozen photographs of our dead President.

There lay *El Comandante* who promised us he'd never die. So the son of a bitch was mortal after all; the one who promised the world tyranny forever was no longer alive to spew forth venomous lies and injustices on our people.

The black and white photograph highlighted the contours of his dead face, his white beard. His cheeks sank into his sallow face pulling his chin upward. This made his beard point up in the most comical way, almost making him look like a gnome instead of the leader of a country. There was peace in his

125

visage. In fact, the dead tyrant looked like a constipated old man who was finally having the bowel movement he had been praying for.

Fidel wasn't wearing his usual green fatigues, but rather a very elegant dark blue or black suit, hard to tell from the black and white image, and he sported a silk tie that was as light as his shirt. The casket was metal instead of mahogany or oak, which surprised me because he looked like he was stuck in a freezer rather than a coffin. The top of the coffin was glass, an inflated bubble covering him from head to toe. Plastic wrap to keep the mango green forever.

A Cuban flag draped over a portion of the refrigerator-like casket, an eternal red-white-and-blue quilt, which flowed over the bottom half of the coffin like ripples of falling water. The black and white photos looked like pictures in a nickelodeon I saw at the fair when I was a kid, the same fair where I first saw the mares at Lenin Park. A man had taken the pictures out of the back of the nickelodeon to show me that they were all almost identical except for one tiny movement, one bat of an eyelash, so the movement would always flow when the pictures were flipped sequentially to add to the realism of the story.

That's how these pictures looked. They were all pretty much the same except for the placement of the flag, which was bunched just a little off in each image. If I had the time, I would've picked up the stack of photos and flicked them through my fingers, the way the man at the fair did, and I would create my own make-shift cartoon of our dead President. There was no doubt that I would see the flag waving back and forth majestically flowing over the corpse's still image.

I wasn't surprised they preserved him like Eva Perón or Lenin, like some fetal pig in a bottle of formaldehyde so people could visit him and flick their fingernails on the side of the bottle to see if the specimen would move.

I realized then he would be viewed only by Raúl and other select party members who must be in on the deception, until the day came when they could no longer expect anyone to believe Fidel was 100 years old. Even in the black and white photo, I could see the wax and makeup dull and almost dusty, powdery. This was the face that was meant to remain in our memories long after his death was announced. This was the face that all loyal revolutionaries would line up outside a yet to be built mausoleum to view. This was the face that was meant to bring us to tears.

My fingers flipped to the next picture in the stack, then the next, then the next. In each, members of *el Partido Comunista*, Raúl, and others dignitaries stood around the coffin staring down at the waxen visage in one photo, then postured solemnly toward the camera in the next. I flipped absently through the pile, nothing changing but the flag and the faces. Then I flipped back. A new face had appeared next to Raúl. A face that was more than familiar. A face that was a ghost. A face that mirrored that in the glass and metal coffin. It was the green mango, not green and putrefying in death, but bright and alive, still clinging to the tree and swinging in the sunshine.

"*Ay Dios mio,*" I muttered more than under my breath.

Nestor responded, "Shh, stay quiet."

Ignoring my cousin's warning to be still, "Castro is dead! Take a look! Castro's standing over his own coffin."

"What do you mean?" Nestor asked, confused.

"How could the President be standing over his own body?" We both stared at the picture.

"These smart sons-of-bitches found a way to keep the President alive even after death. A puppet! They've found a look-alike who's been pretending to be our *Líder*!" Nestor could not contain himself. We both laughed.

"He fooled us so much in life. Now he continues to fool us even in his death," I said incredulously.

Putting the pictures back in the cardboard envelope they were kept in originally, I placed the file in my pants, covering the top part with my damp T-shirt.

"*Ahora sí,*" Nestor mumbled to himself.

"What else? Look, I think we got enough here to..."

"What did you say fissile materials were?" Nestor asked knowing quite well I hadn't defined the term but he was afraid to look stupid. He did the same thing when he met girls who wouldn't give him their names, *and what was your name again?*

127

"I'm not quite sure," I lied. "It's just nuclear waste. Trash."

"So what's the big deal? The Kazakhs are dumping their trash here. Big whoop. Dig a hole and dump it in," my cousin proposed handing me this file to stick in my pants as well; his were already too full with other documents and manila folders.

"Nestor, it's dangerous as hell. You can't just dig a hole. If that stuff seeps into the soil and gets into our water supply, do you know what that would do to us, our livestock, our farms?"

"OK, I get it," was my cousin's way of telling me he wasn't interested. "Well, it seems that they're paying us to dump this stuff here – makes the Russians look good worldwide when the rest of the world goes and checks out their progress – and they're paying us in drugs. They're bringing both on the same shipment – nuclear waste and the stuff. Pretty good deal, don't you think? Let me bury my trash here, sir, and I'll give you all the junk you wish."

"I'm not sure it's that simple, Nestor. I think the Colombians are involved." I was about to continue, "I still don't understand why the Americans don't blow the lid on this whole thing," when a voice behind us spoke.

"Pues mira lo que tenemos aquí," I heard from outside the office. A soldier with an AK-47 stood there snickering, his nostrils and upper lip flaring, his eyes blinking awfully fast. My heart dropped and I lost feeling in my legs, right down to my little pinky toe.

"Nestor!" I screamed as the soldier came in with two others who seemed just as high on the *yeyo* as the first guy. They probably found some lying around during the hubbub of the blinking lights and helped themselves to a few lines.

Nestor looked at me with his eyes as wide as ever. He didn't have to say a word. It would have been bad enough to get caught in the truck or even outside the factory. But to get caught in here rummaging through files was as ill-fated as it could get. I wondered if they knew the President was dead. Maybe we could barter the files in return for our freedom.

"¿Oye, qué pasa?" my cousin tried to use his charm to get out of the office.

128

Smack! One of the soldiers broke Nestor's nose with the butt of the AK-47. Blood sprayed my T-shirt and on some of the files still sitting on the table. The spastic soldiers grabbed us and began to walk us down to the main platform. One of them grabbed me by the neck. I quickly reached into my pocket and threw a handful of the red-and-black *eleke* beads on the floor, pretending the guard had just torn my blessed necklace from my neck.

Knowing how superstitious my *compañeros* could be with things like these, "Look what you did! You broke my *eleke!*"

"*¡No!*" the guard who had me by the neck screamed, my cousin still dazed from his broken nose. The guard knew what it meant to tear off beads that had the *Orísha's* blessings. He wiped his hands on his green uniform, hoping this gesture would clean away any bad luck he just brought his way.

The lights began blinking again and the soldiers just stood there, jerking their necks like startled birds, too many stimuli for their drug- and adrenaline-filled bodies. A few more blinks and everything was dark and quiet. Before the generators had time to come on, Nestor and I took advantage of the situation and sprinted towards the creaky metal stairs that now sounded like a broken tambourine due to the pouncing of our feet.

My mind was going faster than I could register, but my feet seemed to be doing a graceful *pas-de-deux*. "Run!" I screamed, not so much at Nestor as much as I was commanding my feet to follow suit. And that's when the world just stopped. I felt even *los santos* stop their bickering for a millisecond.

I'm not sure if I felt or heard the shot first. But a bullet scraped my left bicep and went right into Nestor's back who was a few steps ahead. It was like watching a slow-motion movie at El Cine Yara or the nickelodeon at Lenin Park. Nestor's head whiplashed back, his eyes closed. I saw his mouth agape as if he were about to say something, but he fell even before he could scream.

"No!" I heard myself shout, still in slow motion, "No!" Everything at the factory stopped when the shot reverberated off the walls.

People were running in every direction downstairs, still not certain from where the shot came. Most ran outside, dropping bottles of clear liquid or whatever it was they carried. The three soldiers ran up to me as I tried to slap my cousin Nestor out of it.

"C'mon!" I smacked his limp body. "C'mon!"

As I knelt over my cousin, his body smelling of blood and gunpowder, I saw two wing-tip shoes in front of me. Must've been powerful wing-tips because the soldiers stopped dead in their tracks and moved away from me.

"I'll take this from here," Mr. Mendelsen ordered. The soldiers didn't move. "I said I'll handle it! Scram!" The soldiers didn't understand what scram meant, but they understood Mr. Mendelsen wanted them out of there. They bumped into each other trying to find a way downstairs without crossing Mr. Mendelsen, my dead cousin, or me.

"They killed him," I whispered to the American. "He's just a kid and they killed him!" I don't know why I was pleading with a man who I thought was evil; there was just no one else there to plead with.

Nestor's spilt blood attached itself to the grids that made up the metal floor, forming multidirectional square pools that then separated into smaller pools and even smaller pools until the entire upstairs floor was one huge network of Nestor's blood making new patterns around his body, like red moss on the cracks of a sidewalk.

"We gotta get out of here, Ulises."

"What? No, I can't leave him," I told Mr. Mendelsen. "I can't leave my cousin. Maybe a doctor, maybe my stepfather."

"Uli, he's gone. And if you ever want to see your mom and dad again you'll do what I say."

"Antonio's not my dad! My dad's dead!" I shouted, not understanding why I was yelling at Mr. Mendelsen about my father's death, something he clearly had nothing to do with. Tears rolled down my cheeks as I sat there unwilling to believe

130

what had just happened. Maybe this was a dream. Maybe this was all a dream and I would soon wake up to *Jirafa* or *El Enamora'o* fighting over the Vietnamese magazine.

CHAPTER 16

"We gotta go now!" Mr. Mendelsen insisted, grabbing me and pulling a gun out of his holster. "And if you saw those files you're carrying, you now know your father, Ulises, is not dead but working with us back in the States."

"No! You bastard. *¡Hijo de puta!* My father's dead. He visits me at night and is hurt that my mother remarried. He isn't a spy. You have no right to even whisper his name. Do you hear me? You have no right."

Mr. Mendelsen working with Castro's brother, our Vice-President, my stepfather, and now my real father was alive? This was too much reality for a few weeks. Too much unfiltered light. Mr. Mendelsen was part of the Underground that wanted to destroy my country. Yet, he held me back and acted as my aegis while we found a way out of the factory.

"I know who you are," I whispered.

"You don't even know the half of it if you still think your father is dead," the American responded while looking around to see if anyone was approaching. "He saved my ass many times, and I need to return the favor by saving yours!"

Workers and soldiers were still running in every direction, and Mr. Mendelsen pulled me out of the factory through a back door right under the office. Like a well-rehearsed drill, all the armored trucks containing the fissile materials sped out of the factory one behind the other until that side of the factory was bereft of everything except the oil stains on the floor of the garage and loading docks.

I looked up and saw my cousin lying there. It wasn't so much that he was dead. Well, I take that back, Nestor being dead

132

was something I would never get over. What I mean is that I just left him all alone. Lying there, bleeding. He wouldn't have left me behind.

"We gotta go back and get him. Please, Mr. Mendelsen. That's my best friend in the whole wide world."

"Not now, Ulises. Just stay low," the *yanqui* demanded. "Give me the files you have."

Ignoring his command, "I can't just leave him like that," I sniveled, "no matter what happens to me."

"I'll come back for him, I swear. But we need to get you out of here before they realize what just happened. I must take you to your father, so please give me those files! I know this is a lot to handle right now, but if you're anything like your father, you're a survivor. So, c'mon now! They're going to expect me to help them investigate what's happening. I've got no time! And I promised to keep you safe."

We hurried toward the shore. No men were outside protecting the factory from the storm; there were clearly other priorities. The men who led the armored trucks far away from Tarará were back inside now joining the frenzy.

"What did you see? What do you know?" The American asked as we ran away from the factory. He looked around feigning composure. "I need to know what you know. Just give me those damn files. Tell me what you know, Ulises."

I looked into his eyes and lied, "Nothing." If Nestor and his movies had taught me anything was that when someone with a gun, a *yanqui* no less, asks you what you know, you make it clear you know nothing. "I just took these files but didn't read any of them. I have no idea what's going on here."

"I somehow doubt that," Mr. Mendelsen said, looking around the shore, trying to find a way of escape from Tarará. "You seem wilier than that. What files do you have there, Ulises?" Mr. Mendelsen asked again matter-of-factly. "I'm not going to ask again."

It scared me how he tried to manipulate his voice to make me think he wasn't nervous, that he posed no threat. Even at a time like this, when I would've been more comforted to see him panic than keep his cool, Mr. Mendelsen had enough

133

stillness about him that he could manipulate his voice so that I didn't think he was as scared as I was.

Grabbing the files out from under my shirt, "OK, so you know more than most people would feel comfortable you knowing. But a promise is a promise."

I learned in school that in the guise of morality, Americans always fomented trouble in countries that didn't fit the political scheme of things. Is this what was happening? Was it more beneficial for the *yanquis* to keep the world believing that Fidel was still in power? I would think they would give anything to be able to come back on the island and open their casinos, businesses, and other entrepreneurial endeavors as they had decades ago. Moreover, it looked like they had Raúl right where they wanted him.

"Ulises, you think you can make it to that boat over there?" Mr. Mendelsen pointed, his blond locks now a wet mousy brown pasted against his pink skin. It was raining harder than before, thundering louder than it was earlier, and I could hardly understand him as he was speaking English too quickly.

I looked at the small Yamaha fishing boat bumping furiously against the pier. "Yeah, you want me to hide there?" I asked knowing that as soon as I had the chance I would run back into the woods, away from Mr. Mendelsen and back to my troupe.

"He's not going anywhere, Señor Mendelsen," one of Castro's main henchmen shouted in the rain. "Why are you helping this young boy who clearly tried to sabotage our operation?" the bald man asked, his chin jutting out as if challenging the stormy sky, as if challenging *Changó* himself.

"Helping this little piece of shit?" Mr. Mendelsen laughed, looking down at me and offering me a small wink to let me know tacitly that he was really on my side, really there to protect me.

"Seems like that to me. Let's come this way, out of the storm," the bald man gesticulated ever so politely.

Like an American cowboy who must've done this a zillion times, Mr. Mendelsen pulled his gun and shot the bald man right in the head. It was that easy. I started heading off to the boat as Mr. Mendelsen pulled me closer to him.

"I hope you don't mind a little company, Ulises," the American said as he led me to the boat. "It's now you and me, kid. I can't go back in there."

"Where are we going?"

"To see your father. Then to your new home. You can't stay here! You're coming with me to America."

"America?" I asked astonished, "I can't leave my mother."

But Mr. Mendelsen ignored me as we ran toward the pier where the blue and white Yamaha fandangoed on the waves. Everything was happening too fast. Men were yelling that they heard shots fired behind the factory. Green uniforms would swarm this area soon like locusts. Was my father truly alive? Was he waiting for me? What about Graciela? She couldn't know all of this. She'd certainly die from shock.

"Jump in and keep your head down!" Mr. Mendelsen ordered.

"But we gotta get Nestor. I can't leave him."

The port side of the boat was being sprayed with bullets from soldiers who knew they couldn't let us get away. I was hoping this was some type of 007 bullet-proof boat and we'd speed off leaving the soldiers kicking themselves on shore like a bunch of stooges. But that wasn't the case.

"They're going for the gas tank!" I shouted. I had seen this in a movie once and knew that the boat would blow up in seconds.

"What?" Mr. Mendelsen shouted trying to start the boat, but the engine just neighed like old mares.

"The gas tank!" I shouted, standing up so Mr. Mendelsen could hear me.

"No!" Mr. Mendelsen shouted, gesturing to stay down.

The men didn't rush us as I'd expect. Instead, they continued moving in, their ammunition nowhere near running out.

"Ah," I heard, not knowing if it was the engine or Mr. Mendelsen. The American's face turned pale, his lips purple. He

135

took a bullet that could've easily been mine. His eyes glazed over as if he no longer cared whether we escaped or not. In fact, he looked relieved that it was all over for him. He reached under one of the seats and grabbed a nylon bag that contained a briefcase. With a bullet in his chest, he took the files I had and stuck them into the nylon bag.

"Zip it up," he let out in agony. "Zip...the bag...give it to your father."

"My father?"

"Yes! Make sure Antonio gets this to your father. Take it," he moaned trying to shake off the pain. "Ulises," Mr. Mendelsen was now bent over, holding his heart. "Take this to your house. Give it to Antonio, before they realize who you are. Take it!"

"What do you mean?" I asked, hoping he wouldn't die on me before explaining what was going on. Had I heard correctly? He wanted my stepfather to give it to my father? Maybe he meant for me to tell my father what was going on in one of my dreams when my father appeared to me, but that didn't make much sense at all. I held the sealed bag in my arms like a football. Mr. Mendelsen continued pushing me away toward the rear of the boat.

"What're you doing?" I urged. "Just sit there. I'll start the boat, and you can give this to my stepfather yourself. I don't want anything to do with this."

"There's no time," he gasped. "Push me off the boat."

"No, I'm not going to do to you what you did to Zyrena, what they did to Nestor."

Trying not to laugh because it hurt so much, Mr. Mendelsen whispered, "Nestor was an innocent bystander in all this, but Zyrena..." he coughed more and more blood. "Zyrena killed many, many men with her silky voice."

"Can't be!"

"Just do it! Push me off the boat and go. Go!"

I reached down trying to keep from getting my head blown off. With Mr. Mendelsen's help, I rolled him off the stern, where the motor now puttered with very little gas.

The splash spit cold ocean water on my face, waking me up for at least a few more minutes. If I had only known that I would never set foot on my island's dry land, I would've probably jumped in the water with the dead *yanqui*.

The Yamaha puttered away from the coast, out into the open ocean, not knowing where I would go, not knowing how I could live with what I had experienced that night. I kept thinking of Nestor lying back there all alone. I didn't think too much of Mr. Mendelsen, except that his words kept ringing in my ears.

I needed to get back home to tell everyone what happened, to tell them where Nestor's remains lay.

Boom! I looked back at the sound of a shattering explosion, wondering if people were after me shooting grenades or something. Off in the distant shore of Tarará, an orange mushroom cloud brightened the tropical sky. There were two smaller explosions after the main one that crescendoed like a Rachmaninoff etude, adding to the spectacle. So much for evidence, so much for getting Nestor out.

CHAPTER 17

The Yamaha crawled through the ocean, the shoreline still in sight. I looked for the bag, and it was still aboard. I needed proof, wherever I ended up, that this all occurred. Everything was already getting fuzzy in my head.

I wasn't sure if I even knew Nestor was really dead.

I thought of how I'd explain all of this to my mother, my aunt and uncle – Nestor's parents – and how my stepfather would react to my knowing so much.

I kept my mind busy to avoid thinking how far I had sailed or how exhausted I was. So many pointless deaths. But Nestor's wasn't going to be that way. By the time I was through with telling his story – in the true tall-tale manner so fitting to my cousin – they'd be building statues of him everywhere. I pictured his first statue. Would it be at the Marina Hemingway or right in Tarará where he died?

My lungs hurt from the heavy panting. I was starting to hyperventilate and knew I had to calm down or I would pass out. It felt like my lungs would soon burst like over-inflated balloons. You would think the Caribbean at night would be as warm and alive as it was during the day, but the reality was that it was frigid and lifeless and smelled like death. Trying to eyeball a landmark to guide me towards home, I kept the shore in view. Keeping my eyes on details of the shore, my breathing began to slow down.

In order to save the little petrol I had, I shut the motor off. The Yamaha was as obedient to the current paralleling the shore as the mares were to *la virgencita* in my dreams. With water in my ears and fatigue alluring my brain to shut down and

138

sleep, I let myself sink to the boat floor so I could rest – just for a couple minutes.

Falling asleep, or maybe starting to pass out, I started to dream of the mares in Lenin Park. I hardly noticed the putter of a motorboat approaching.

I forced myself to get up and look around, but I couldn't see any boat. I allowed the Yamaha to continue trotting through the water. No one would see me through this approaching fog.

Perhaps it was an audible hallucination. I heard once that people under duress often see and hear things that aren't really there. Attributing the sound of the motorboat to an hallucination, I continued paddling, still viewing the shore with one eye.

A beam of light tore through the blackness, shining close to where the Yamaha idly rocked with the current. Turning around to find whence the light came, wondering if there was some supernatural source lighting my way, I saw a small fishing boat dawdling towards me.

Ready to jump into the water, the boat just passed on by. The old man waving probably thought that I was out illegally fishing for my family or for the black market.

"I was hoping you were a giant school of tuna!" the man laughed as he passed me, the lull in his voice giving away that he was inebriated, probably just drunk on homemade *aguardiente*.

I kept the bag I carried tight in my grip, ready to jump any second. The old man chugged from the thermos as he passed me, grimacing at the taste of the warm liquid. Obviously, the thermos contents made the irony of our existence less cruel.

The murmur of the motor boat gliding into the fog, the Yamaha slowly rocking back and forth behind him, more and more distance between us, lulled me to sleep, and as much as I tried to keep my eyes open, they were as heavy as the pain I felt in my heart.

I dreamed of Fortuna singing that song of hers, the one of the artist forgetting to paint black angels. It was the deepest sleep I have ever had, just dreaming of Fortuna and the camp. No mares. No dead Nestor or Zyrena. Just peace.

139

Yawning, I opened my eyes half expecting to wake up at home or with Troupe 476. The yawn jolted me, though, as I saw I was on the boat, alone.

In front of me, I was finally catching up to the rolling white fog coming head-on. *Easy, easy*, I thought, trying to coax the fog into not engulfing the Yamaha. But the fog was deaf to my request. I continued dillydallying with no motor on towards what seemed like Cojimar. I tried the motor again, but this time it was to no avail. Chug. Chug. The motor had either finally died or I used the last of the petrol as the motor choked.

The white cloud swallowed me up with no regard – as if I were only a figment of its imagination, as if I were only a part of a dream it was having while it rolled over the shallows. I sat dead still, frozen with fear. First, the bow of the boat disappeared and then my entire being was gone. My hands were just shadows that I waved in front of me to test the fog's thickness.

"Take it slow. C'mon. Slow," I whispered, not wanting the fog to know I was trying to rush home. Was I dreaming? Was I really still asleep and only thought I was awake? At times, it felt as if I weren't moving at all, like if I were just lying still, run over by the fog.

I wished Nestor were here. He would've known what to do, known what to say to make me feel less lonesome and scared. It seemed like weeks had passed since I was fleeing from the factory with Mr. Mendelsen, months since I had seen Nestor's dead body, when in reality it had just occurred. Maybe all that hadn't really happened. Perhaps I was still in my bunk at the compulsory work camp watching everyone play canasta.

I need to get closer to shore, I thought confidently, trying to sound like Nestor.

I was losing perspective. I much rather have risked hitting the shore than heading off into nothingness. My fear was palpable, and I didn't want the fog to feel that. Would *Yemayá* keep me in this fog forever? *Yemayá* loved her seafarers and often didn't let them go, nobody hearing from them again. But no, this was just fog. Just fog. Besides, the fog was getting lower and lower, now just grazing the boat. I tried to keep my eyes on the now visible power lines about a quarter kilometer away. I

140

believed if I continued parallel to the shore, if the Yamaha continued with the current, I would eventually see lights of a town and I could jump off with my impermeable bag of evidence that needed to get to my father.

The boat just drifted into emptiness, and I saw the current was taking me closer to shore. I knew this because natural and man-made trash began to hit the side of the Yamaha.

Drifting green coconut husks took on the shape of decapitated heads; cans and wrappers from the tourist beaches looked like shrapnel. I tried not to look at any one shape too long, hoping these images would disappear, but they didn't. Three palm trees hunched over on the shore looked like three old ladies over a boiling cauldron, fronds outstretched with what looked like bats ready to be dropped in their witch's brew. I even glanced overboard at what looked like Nestor's dead body, but it was only half an abandoned lobster crate that one of the tourist hotels must've lost.

"Suave, suave," I whispered again. This time I was sure the fog could hear me. Although I still couldn't see much in front of me, I felt sure that the white cloud would spit me free soon. I heard someone take a deep breath and then realized it was I falling asleep again, being lulled by the waves hitting the sides of the boat and by the fog's rhythm that seemed to be synchronized now to the waves.

I forced myself to stay awake. Not because I was afraid of where the current would take me as much as afraid of the dreams I would have. I had had enough dreaming, enough illusions for one evening.

A few buzzards faced the water. These birds once flourished on the wooded parts of the island, staying on land for any scrap of food. But we took over their duties as scavengers and left them nothing, no rodents, no small birds, nothing. We even hunted some of these buzzards when our bellies really rumbled.

Nestor said they tasted like pork, but that their flesh smelled like rotting meat when you were cooking them, so it was best to stew them for a long time. When cooking these birds, windows remained open like when cooking *bacalao.* The

141

scavenger birds still survived on our island, though. They simply moved to the shore and picked on dead fish or hermit crabs. Maybe they simply moved closer to shore, finding a haven on these power lines, to get away from us.

I blinked several times to try to focus on the trek back home, forcing myself to stay awake. I reached over portside to splash water on my face. The salt on my lips tasted good. The cold water helped me sort out the night's events into neat categories of illusion and reality.

Sleep, nevertheless, came and draped me as I rocked back and forth on the boat. When I would awaken, there would be no land to be seen.

CHAPTER 18

I could hear the power lines far away buzzing as they usually did after a good rainfall. The buzzing was as loud and as fast as the thoughts that ran through my head, the panic that sped through my veins as I slept, as I dreamed of my mother, Graciela, mopping the mud and dirt caked in the corners of the screened-in porch that Nestor and I helped my uncle build years ago.

I could see in her face that she wanted to be extra clean, her arms gripping the timeworn towel and four-foot *frasada,* a wooden stick that Cubans, whether in exile or still on the island I discovered, used to mop anything from wooden floors to ceramic tile. Like a pendulum, methodical and effective, Graciela's strokes swished to and fro.

As in most dreams, people change. Graciela suddenly turned into buck-toothed Beatriz and ran inside the house. *I have to open the shades,* Beatriz thought. Who knows who's watching the house and having closed shades with this heat means we're hiding something.

Now back to Graciela in her wedding dress, my mother looked around searching for inventive ways to bring sunlight into our shadowy abode, hoping to vent the damp smell that had come in from all the rains and the stagnant water from the clogged drains.

My mother gave up trying to figure out why our home didn't welcome sunlight this time of year the way the other homes in the neighborhood did or why our home trapped smells and odors regardless of how often she vacuumed the carpet with the odor-eliminating and fragrance powder from relatives in Miami that promised to get rid of even the toughest cigar and pet smells. Certainly, if this American deodorizer didn't work, nothing would.

The lack of illumination had to be attributed to the way the city block was engineered, she figured. Or it must've been the way our home sat where El Vedado bordered Miramar. A Cuban flaw, maybe even a material dialectic.

I knew my mother felt that houses in Cuba should all receive the equal share of sunlight, always expel odors out to the Caribbean. "No house of mine should be denied a drink of sunlight while the others gobble it all up!" Graciela stated, quickly realizing she was speaking aloud.

"Mami, why are we leaving? What are the suitcases doing in here?"

Graciela just ignored me as if I were a phantom. I was scared for my mother. Had my disappearing and Nestor being murdered finally driven her over the edge, even in my dreams?

Graciela sat next to our statue of *la virgencita* and jumped from story to story, thought to meaningless tangential thought about the hues in the house, how the dark browns, crimsons, and sapphires present during most of the day were but lighter hues of the usual illusory colors.

"Look at you, *Cachita,*" my mother addressed the statue of Our Lady, her eyes moving fast around the house as if someone unseen whispered a joke in her ear. "Even you, resting there on that *maldito* TV, seem to have changed from your usual golden gown to a more saffron shade. Well," Graciela continued her one-sided conversation with *Cachita,* "everyone needs to make sacrifices during these times, even you, Our Lady herself."

"Mami, you're scaring me. Sit down. I'll get our things."

Graciela still couldn't hear me, or at least just ignored me. This made me angry.

My mother straightened the mirror hanging opposite the Catholic icon, making sure that the Madonna could see how beautiful she looked in the orange-yellow gown, even if it were a darker hue. My grandmother gave Graciela the graven image the day my mother was born. It was a blessed statue. My mother placed a new candle and an orange from the back yard next to

144

the idol every day, as Our Lady always kept the family safe and deserved respect and praise.

Graciela crossed herself after lighting the candle and looked into the golden arabesque mirror, curious how she herself looked this morning. Tactless as ever, the looking glass satiated her intrigue. The newly-formed crevices in her face were becoming deep abysses being formed and manipulated by many years of preoccupation. The closer she looked, the more chasms appeared. She looked like she had aged decades in just a few weeks.

Always full of grace and mercy, however, Our Lady allowed the aroma of the boiling black bean soup to abruptly break my mother's trance.

"¡Los frijoles, madre santísima!" And off she trotted to the kitchen for a careful sniff and stir. Graciela just added dashes of Caribbean spices and herbs, she cradled a bean between her teeth. *Almost*, she thought.

I began sobbing in my dream – deep, cathartic sobs. But Graciela still didn't see or hear me.

The phone rang, and I could hear it was our neighbor, that nosy Maria-Teresa, whom everyone called Maïté. I could tell by my mother's gasping that this would be a short call.

"No, everything's fine. It's just these *frijoles*. You know how it is. We imitate everything our grandmothers used, to the milligram; yet, it just doesn't taste like those beans from when we were kids."

Maïté interrupted with apparently the juiciest story about the Germans who visited her last spring, but Graciela continued talking about the damn bean stew.

"The cumin had more punch when I was a kid; the roasted bell pepper was simply smokier." She winced as she dashed some more garlic salt into the bubbling pot, attempting to precisely recreate her grandmother's recipe.

Our Lady gave her the hope that every time she cooked this Cuban side dish she would eventually reach the right combination and permutation to make everyone's taste buds remember life as kids.

Graciela hung up the phone, not even a good-bye. She continued adding bay leaves, more ground cumin, and a pinch of sugar to the stewing cauldron, praying that this time she had done it. She hoped that the ham shank she purchased on the black market, after a friend of Antonio's euthanized a pig, would add that necessary touch. She lowered the flame. Perhaps the many years of mimicking would sizzle away on a lower flame.

Before waking up and realizing that I would never step foot in Cuba again, never step foot in my black-and-white tiled bedroom, Graciela grabbed the pot of beans and threw it in the backyard, disgusted that her stew didn't taste right.

The mares of Lenin Park, no blinders, no age showing on their long muzzles or coats, galloped toward the pot, licking up every bit – not caring the soup didn't taste quite like those old memories.

CHAPTER 19

I awoke from this dream, and the many other dreams I had those last few days on the water, those last few days of seeing no land anywhere, just porpoises, sharks, and even a tortoise once that looked dizzy as if waking up from a decade's long slumber. The sun beat down on me mercilessly throughout the days out on the Straits of Florida. The waves licked at the sides of my boat almost purposefully.

In the middle of the Straits, I remembered how desperately I left my homeland, clutching nothing but a satchel of secrets. No food. No water. I took nothing tangible from the life I was leaving behind save for thoughts, observations, and memories – some written on scraps of paper in my bag, others etched on my brain. I was succumbing to delirium from lack of water due to those long days and nights I spent floating freely between the water and the sky.

The haze from the heat and the humidity lifted off the surface of the water as I awoke with my head still in a haze. The sounds of the sea were disorienting, louder than thunder. Was *Changó* at it again?

The sea was churning against my boat and I could feel a storm was approaching, the smell of ozone mixed with the salty air reaching my nostrils. I saw the sky turning blue and orange above the railing of my boat and the sounds of waves and thunder turned to voices, both English and Spanish. The waves lapped over the edge of the boat threatening to swamp it. Those waves, though, turned to shapes and forms of light and shadow climbing aboard.

In my delusion I heard a voice, "Uli. Ulises." With the voice came a vision. A vision not of the Virgin Mary, not of *Yemayá* trying to keep me for herself on the ocean, but rather a vision of my father.

"Uli!" I heard my dead father's voice calling as if it were from another universe, as if it were from my regular dreams where his ghost visited me from beyond while I lay restless in my bed back in Havana. His voice came through in surges behind the ringing in my ears, my dehydrated head thumping like the cowbell of a merciless *bongocero* riffing a *montuno*.

"Uli! *Despiértate,* Uli." my father kept calling me, trying to arouse me from my slumber.

I wanted to respond, and thought I knew everything that was going on around me, but I was paralyzed, couldn't move or speak. I lay there lifeless on the small Yamaha boat that made it across the Straits of Florida without any petrol, my fourteen-year-old, sunburned body caked with salt and grime, my blistered lips cracked like the sidewalks in my neighborhood block back in El Vedado.

I heard men and women scurrying around me, one slipping on the wet surface of the Yamaha. Someone stepped on my right arm, which felt as if he crushed it, but I couldn't even whimper with pain.

I kept hearing my father bark orders to everyone while trying to keep composure, but I could hear his voice vacillating from a stern command to a whisper, as if he were about to break down any second. I wondered if his countenance gave him away or if he were as stalwart as he was in the pictures I used to rummage through back home.

Was this really my father, Ulises Aguilera, whom we all thought back in Havana was killed in Angola back in the late seventies, a hero in our country for dying for the causes of the Revolution?

I continued hearing voices like hummingbirds zipping in my ears, including my father's, and felt someone scoop me up in his robust arms. My tight, burned skin felt like it could tear clean off my bones.

148

"Make sure to get him some oxygen, some more fluids. *¡Inmediatamente!*" I heard my father demand from the coast guard who had pulled up beside my boat, my father's voice didn't vacillate this time.

I opened my eyes as much as I could, the sun blinding me, my eyeballs feeling like orbs of sandpaper underneath my eyelids. My long black eyelashes that were so common in Aguilera men were sticky with brine and made it even more difficult to open my eyes. It *was* he!

This was true. This wasn't just another hallucination from my dehydrated brain after spending who knows how long out in the open sea.

It must have just been auspicious that I reached the United States, Fortuna would have said, that the *Orísha* were finally smiling upon me. Perhaps the gods were no longer fighting with one another about everything I had experienced. They must've figured it all out. *Changó* must've settled his differences with the other gods, and *Yemayá* didn't keep me for herself at sea. She kept me safe on that little boat and made sure I was reunited with my father.

The *Orísha* must have considered their bickering imprudent, reckless, and after all that they put me through, after the pain of seeing Nestor die right in front of me at the fábrica right under the hill of our work camp in *Tarará*, after the pain of being forced to leave my mother behind and the only home I ever knew without even being able to say goodbye, they probably figured it was better that I found my way to the U.S., a land that regarded the *Orísha* as mere folly, a land where they were mere mythical shadows projected on the threadbare movie screen of our Cuban memories.

"*Papi?*" I whispered, not sure if I truly made sounds or if I were just speaking in my head. "*Papi?* Is that you?" the sun still blinding me. Was the sun always this bright in America?

I heard a guttural cry from Ulises followed by a gasp that can only come after you stop breathing for a long while, like when Nestor and I used to hold our breath underwater at the public pool in Lenin Park.

"Yes, yes! It's me, Uli."

149

I looked into his face. I was so used to seeing him like he looked in the picture taken before he went to war, the picture that showed a young, vibrant soldier who would do anything for his country, the picture my mother put away when she remarried. But here was the real Ulises, a much more mature man that I realized I didn't know at all, a man with crow's feet and lines on his forehead, a small scar on his defined chin that had healed years ago, and gray strands, barely noticeable, poking through his temples.

"But how?" I choked, my tonsils sticking to the back of my throat. If I had anything left in my system, I would've thrown up for sure. "How are you alive?" The ringing in my ears continued like the calypso drums that played at Marina Hemingway.

"Don't worry about any of that now, Uli. There's nothing for you to worry now that you've reached Miami. You made it, Uli! You made it!" My father was as proud as he could be, as if I had any power, any control over where and when I landed, as if I had really wanted to leave my mother behind.

Ulises kept slapping my face as softly as he could, "Stay with me, Uli. Stay with me, please!"

I cracked a smile hallucinating Nestor and I were roughhousing, slapping each other around for no reason, and my father laughed with gratitude thinking I was conscious, "There you go. We Aguileras don't give up, so don't give up now."

"I won't *Papi*. I won't," I whispered, still feeling alone and scared, already homesick for a home I knew I couldn't return to. Not being able to speak anymore, and not realizing they had already moved me onto the coast guard cutter, I grabbed my father's shoulder firmly, refusing to ever let go.

Fortuna was right, and I finally understood what she meant by all her talk about attachment and disillusionment. Disillusionment is a blessing, sacred, eternal. After all, disillusionment freed me of thought, freed me of idealistic promises that only brought me pain and more loss. Disillusionment resurrected my father, extinguished the shadow puppets of Castro's projections, and even brought grace upon the

150

mares of Lenin Park whose blinders blew away like tattered dreams in the night.

ABOUT THE AUTHOR

Agustin D. Martinez was raised in Miami, Florida. He is a graduate of Florida State University and received his Master of Science in Education degree from Johns Hopkins University. His fiction and plays have appeared in *Arcadia Literary Journal, The Binnacle, The 34th Parallel Magazine, The Write Room, Apropos Literary Journal, The Adirondack Review, Press 1, Sugar Mule, Palooka Journal, Review Americana,* and *Hinchas de Poesia.* He lives in the Washington, DC metro area.

www.ingramcontent.com/pod-product-compliance
Lightning Source LLC
Chambersburg PA
CBHW020643250626
47154CB00008B/2785